"Can you think of any reason your stepmother would be so upset about talking to me about the case?"

She shook her head, took a gulp and looked over at him. "You can't really think that she is somehow involved." When he didn't speak instantly, she snapped, "James, my stepmother wouldn't hit a child and keep going."

"I'm not saying she did. But she might know who did."

Lori shook her head, drained her paper cup and set it on the edge of his desk as she rose. "You really think she would keep a secret like that?"

"People keep secrets from those they love all the time," he said.

She glared at him. "What is that supposed to mean?"

"Just that she might be covering for someone."

Her eyes flared. "If you tell me that you think she's covering for me—"

He stood, raising both hands in surrender as he did. "I'm not accusing you. I'm just saying..." He met her gaze, surprised at how hard this was. He and Lori had gone through school together and hardly said two words the entire time. It wasn't like that much had changed over the past few days, he told himself, even as he knew it had. He liked her. Always had.

MURDER GONE COLD

New York Times Bestselling Author
B.J. DANIELS

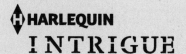

HARLEQUIN
INTRIGUE

This new Intrigue series is dedicated to all my fans who have
followed my books from Cardwell Ranch to Whitehorse and
back again. I hope you like these wild Colt brothers and
Lonesome, Montana.

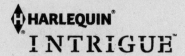

**Recycling programs
for this product may
not exist in your area.**

ISBN-13: 978-1-335-48949-4

Murder Gone Cold

Copyright © 2022 by Barbara Heinlein

This edition published by arrangement with Harlequin Books S.A.

For questions and comments about the quality of this book,
please contact us at CustomerService@Harlequin.com.

Harlequin Enterprises ULC
22 Adelaide St. West, 41st Floor
Toronto, Ontario M5H 4E3, Canada
www.Harlequin.com

Printed in U.S.A.

B.J. Daniels is a *New York Times* and *USA TODAY* bestselling author. She wrote her first book after a career as an award-winning newspaper journalist and author of thirty-seven published short stories. She lives in Montana with her husband, Parker, and three springer spaniels. When not writing, she quilts, boats and plays tennis. Contact her at bjdaniels.com, on Facebook or on Twitter, @bjdanielsauthor.

Books by B.J. Daniels

Harlequin Intrigue

A Colt Brothers Investigation

Murder Gone Cold

Cardwell Ranch: Montana Legacy

Steel Resolve
Iron Will
Ambush Before Sunrise
Double Action Deputy
Trouble in Big Timber
Cold Case at Cardwell Ranch

Whitehorse, Montana: The Clementine Sisters

Hard Rustler
Rogue Gunslinger
Rugged Defender

HQN

Montana Justice

Restless Hearts
Heartbreaker
Heart of Gold

Visit the Author Profile page at Harlequin.com.

CAST OF CHARACTERS

James "Jimmy D" Colt—The handsome rodeo cowboy is back home in Lonesome, Montana, banged up and down on his luck—until he bunks in his father's old private detective office and finds both trouble and true love.

Lorelei "Lori" Wilkins—Her sandwich shop business is going great and so is her life—until Jimmy D Colt moves in to the building next to hers and begins investigating a cold case that hits too close to home.

Del Colt—James's father was killed before he could solve his last case involving a hit-and-run.

Billy Sherman—The boy saw something out his window. Otherwise, why would a seven-year-old afraid of the dark go outside alone in a thunderstorm? Someone ran down the seven-year-old one dark rainy night and got away with it—until now.

Alice Sherman—She's spent years trying to live with the loss of her son. The last thing she wants is James digging it all back up.

Senator Fred Bayard—He definitely has something to hide other than his girlfriend, but is it an old hit-and-run murder?

Karen Wilkins—Lori's stepmother is neck-deep in the old mystery, and with James's help, Lori plans to get to the bottom of it—even if it's murder.

Sheriff Carl Osterman—Carl and his brother, former sheriff Otis Osterman, had hoped to never see any of the Colt brothers again. How long before James finds out just how dangerous it is to follow in his father's footsteps?

Shelby Crane—She'd do anything to keep her son Todd from being dragged into the hit-and-run case of his once best friend Billy.

Cora Brooks—The older woman liked to spy on people and use what she learned to her advantage. She knew one day it might get her into trouble. Apparently that day has come.

Prologue

Billy Sherman lay in his bed trembling with fear as the thunderstorm raged outside. At a loud crack of thunder, he closed his eyes tight. His mother had warned him about the coming storm. She'd suggested he might want to stay in her room now that his father lived somewhere else.

"Mom, I'm seven," he'd told her. It was bad enough that he still slept with a night-light. "I'll be fine." But just in case, he'd pulled out his lucky pajamas even though they were getting too small.

Now he wished he could run down the hall to her room and crawl into her bed. But he couldn't. He wouldn't. He had to face his fears. That's what his dad said.

Lightning lit up the room for an instant. His eyes flew open to find complete blackness. His night-light had gone out. So had the little red light on his alarm clock. The storm must have knocked out the electricity.

He jumped out of bed to stand at his window. Even the streetlamps were out. He could barely see the house across the street through the pouring rain. He tried to swallow the lump in his throat. Maybe he should run down the hall and tell his mother about the power going off. He knew she would make him stay in her room if he did.

Billy hated being afraid. He dreamed of being strong and invincible. He dreamed of being a spy who traveled the world, solved mysteries and caught bad guys.

His battery-operated two-way radio squawked, making him jump. Todd, his best friend. "Are you asleep?" Todd's voice sounded funny. Billy had never confided even to his best friend about his fear of the dark and storms and whatever might be hiding in his closet. But maybe Todd was scared sometimes too.

He picked up the headset and stepped to the window to look out at the street. "I'm awake." A bolt of lightning blinded him for a moment and he almost shrieked as it illuminated a dark figure, walking head down on the edge of the road in the rain. Who was that and...? He felt his heart leap to his throat. What was it the person was carrying?

Suddenly, he knew what he had to do. He wasn't hiding in his room being scared. He would be strong and invincible. He had a mystery to solve. "I have to go," he said into the headset. "I saw someone. I'm going to follow whoever it is."

"No, it's storming. Don't go out. Billy, don't. Billy?"

He grabbed his extra coat his mother kept on the hook by his door and pulled on his snow-boots. At the window, he almost lost his nerve. He could barely see the figure. If he didn't go now he would never know. He would lose his nerve. He would always be afraid.

He picked up the headset again. "The person is headed down your street. Watch for me. I'll see you in a minute." Opening his window, he was driven back for a moment by the rain and darkness. Then he was through the window, dropping into the shrubbery outside as he'd done so many other times when he and Todd were playing their game. Only the other times, it hadn't been storming or dark.

He told himself that spies didn't worry about a thunderstorm. Spies were brave. But he couldn't wait until he reached Todd's house. Putting his head down he ran through the rain, slowing only when he spotted the figure just ahead.

He'd been breathing hard, his boots slapping the pavement, splashing through the puddles. But because of the storm the person hadn't heard him, wouldn't know anyone was following. That's what always made the game so much fun, spying on people and they didn't even know it.

Billy realized that he wasn't scared. His father had been right, though he didn't understand why his mother had gotten so angry with his dad for telling him to face his fears and quit being such a baby. Billy was facing down the storm, facing down the darkness, facing down all of his fears tonight. He couldn't wait to tell Todd.

He was smiling to himself, proud, when the figure ahead of him suddenly stopped and looked back. In a flash of lightning Billy saw the face under the hooded jacket—and what the person was carrying and screamed.

Nine years later

Chapter One

Cora Brooks stopped washing the few dinner dishes she'd dirtied while making her meal, dried her hands and picked up her binoculars. Through her kitchen window, she'd caught movement across the ravine at the old Colt place. As she watched, a pickup pulled in through the pines and stopped next to the burned-out trailer. She hoped it wasn't "them druggies" who'd been renting the place from Jimmy D's girlfriend—before their homemade meth-making lab blew it up.

The pickup door swung open. All she saw at first was the driver's Stetson as he climbed out and limped over to the burned shell of the double-wide. It wasn't until he took off his hat to rake a hand through his too-long dark hair that she recognized him. One of the Colt brothers, the second oldest, she thought. James Dean Colt or Jimmy D as everyone called him.

She watched him through the binoculars as he hobbled around the trailer's remains, stooping at one point to pick up something before angrily hurling it back into the heap of charred debris.

"Must have gotten hurt with that rodeoin' of his agin,"

she said, pursing her lips in disapproval as she took in his limp. "Them boys." They'd been wild youngins who'd grown into wilder young men set on killing themselves by riding anything put in front of them. The things she'd seen over the years!

She watched him stand there for a moment as if not knowing what to do now, before he ambled back to his pickup and drove off. Putting down her binoculars, she chuckled to herself. "If he's upset about his trailer, wait until he catches up to his girlfriend."

Cora smiled and went back to washing her dishes. At her age, with all her aches and pains, the only pleasure she got anymore was from other people's misfortunes. She'd watched the Colt clan for years over there on their land. Hadn't she said no good would ever come of that family? So far her predictions had been exceeded.

Too bad about the trailer blowing up though. In recent years, the brothers had only used the double-wide as a place to drop their gear until the next rodeo. It wasn't like any of them stayed more than a few weeks before they were off again.

So where was James Dean Colt headed now? Probably into town to find his girlfriend since she'd been staying in his trailer when he'd left for the rodeo circuit. At least she had been—until she'd rented the place out, pocketed the cash and moved back in with her mother. More than likely he was headed to Melody's mother's right now.

What Cora wouldn't have given to see *that* reunion, she thought with a hearty cackle.

Just to see his face when Melody gave him the news after him being gone on the road all these months.

Welcome home, Jimmy D.

JAMES HIGHTAILED IT into the small Western town of Lonesome, Montana. When he'd seen the trailer in nothing but ashes, he'd had one terrifying thought. Had Melody been in it when the place went up in flames? He quickly assured himself that if that had happened, he would have heard about it.

So…why hadn't he heard about the fire? Why hadn't Melody let him know? They'd started dating only a week before he'd left. What they'd had was fun, but definitely not serious for either of them.

He swore under his breath, recalling the messages from her that he hadn't bothered with. All of them were along the line of, "We need to talk. Jimmy D, this is serious. Call me." No man jumped to answer a message like that.

Still, you would think that she could have simply texted him. "About your trailer?" Or "Almost died escaping your place."

At the edge of the small mountain town, he turned down a side street, driving back into the older part of town. Melody's mother owned the local beauty shop, Gladys's Beauty Emporium. Melody worked there doing nails. Gladys had been widowed as long as James could remember. It was one reason Melody always ended up back at her mother's between boyfriends.

He was relieved to see her old Pontiac parked out front of the two-story rambling farmhouse. A spindly stick of a woman with a wild head of bleached curly platinum hair, Gladys Simpson opened the door at his knock. She had a cigarette in one hand and a beer in the other. She took one look at him, turned and yelled, "Mel... Someone here to see you."

Someone? Lonesome was small enough that he could easily say that Gladys had known him his whole life. He waited on the porch since he hadn't been invited in, which was fine with him. He'd been toying with the idea that Melody was probably mad at him. He could think of any number of reasons.

But mad enough to burn down the double-wide out of spite? He'd known some women who could get that angry, but Melody wasn't one of them. He'd seen little passion in her before he'd left. He'd gotten the impression she wasn't that interested in him. If he'd had to guess, he'd say she'd been using him that week to make someone else jealous.

Which was another reason he'd known their so-called relationship wasn't going anywhere. In retrospect though, leaving her to take care of the place had been a mistake. It hadn't been his idea. She'd needed a place to stay. The double-wide was sitting out there empty so she'd suggested watching it for him while he was gone.

Even at the time, he'd worried that it would give her the wrong idea. The wrong idea being that their relationship was more serious than it was. He'd half hoped all the way home that she'd moved back in with her mom or a friend. That the trailer would be empty.

He just never imagined that there would be no place to come home to.

"Jimmy D?"

From the edge of the porch, he turned at the sound of her voice. She stood behind the door, peering around it as if half-afraid of him. "Melody, I was just out at the place. I was worried that you might have gotten caught in the fire."

She shook her head. "I wasn't living there anymore when it happened."

"That's good." But even as he said it, he knew there was more story coming. She was still half hiding behind the door, as if needing a barrier between them. "I'm not angry with you, if that's what you're worried about. I'm just glad you're okay."

He watched her swallow before she said, "I'd rented your trailer to some guys." He took that news without reacting badly. He figured she must have needed the money and he *had* left her in charge of the place, kind of.

"Turned out they were cooking meth," she said. "I didn't know until they blew the place up."

James swallowed back the first few words that leaped to his tongue. When he did find his voice, he said, "You didn't know."

She shook her head. "I didn't." She sounded close to tears. "But that's not all I have to tell you."

He held his breath already fearing that the news wasn't going to get better. Before his grandmother died, she'd explained karma to him. He had a feeling karma was about to kick his butt.

Then Mel stepped around the edge of the door, leading with her belly, which protruded out a good seven months.

The air rushed out of him on a swear word. A million thoughts galloped through his mind at breakneck speed before she said, "It's not yours."

He felt equal parts relief and shock. It was that instant of denial followed by acceptance followed by regret that surprised him the most. For just a second he'd seen himself holding a two-year-old little girl with his dark hair and blue eyes. They'd been on the back of the horse he'd bought her.

When he blinked, the image was gone as quickly as it had come to him.

"Who?" The word came out strangled. He wasn't quite over the shock.

"Tyler Grange," she said, placing her palms on the stretchy top snug over her belly. "He and I broke up just before you and I..." She shrugged and he noticed the tiny diamond glinting on her ring finger.

"You're getting married. When?"

"Soon," she said. "It would be nice to get hitched before the baby comes."

He swallowed, still tangled up in that battle of emotions. Relief was winning by a horse length though. "Congratulations. Or is it best wishes? I never can remember."

"Thanks," she said shyly. "Sorry 'bout your trailer. I'd give you the money I got from the renters, but—"

"It's all right." He took a step toward the porch stairs. After all these years in the rodeo game, he'd learned to cut his losses. This one felt like a win. He swore on his lucky boots that he was going to change his wild ways.

From inside the house, he could hear Gladys laughing with someone. He caught the smell of permanent solution.

"Mama's doing the neighbor's hair," Melody said. He nodded and took a step off the porch. "Any idea where you're going to go?"

Until that moment, he hadn't really thought about it. It wasn't like he didn't have options. He had friends he could bunk with until he either bought another trailer to put on the property or built something more substantial. He and his brothers, also on the rodeo circuit, used the trailer only to stay in the few times they came home to crash for a while—usually to heal up.

Not that he was planning on staying that long. Once he was all healed up from his last rodeo ride, he'd be going back. He'd left his horse trailer, horse and gear at a friend's.

"I'm going to stay at the office," he said, nodding to himself. It seemed the perfect solution under the circumstances.

"Uptown?" she asked, sounding surprised. The word hardly described downtown Lonesome, Montana. But the office *was* at the heart of town—right on a corner of Main Street.

"Don't worry about me," he said. "You just take care of yourself and give my regards to Tyler." He tipped his hat and headed to his pickup.

As he drove away, he realized his heart was still pounding. He'd dodged a bullet. So why couldn't he get that image of him holding his baby daughter out of his head? Worse was how that image made him feel— happy.

The emotion surprised him. For just that split second, he'd had to deal with the thought of settling down, of having a family, of being a father. He'd felt it to his soul and now he missed it.

James shook his head, telling himself that he was just tired, injured and emotionally drained after his home-coming. All that together would make any man have strange thoughts.

Chapter Two

James reached high on the edge of the transom over the door for the key, half-surprised it was still there. He blew the dust off and, opening the door, hit the light switch and froze. The smell alone reminded him of his father and the hours he'd spent in this office as a child after his mother had died.

Later he'd hung around, earning money by helping any way he could at the office. He'd liked hanging out here with his old man. He chuckled, remembering how he'd thought he might grow up and he and Del would work together. Father and son detective agency. Unfortunately, his father's death had changed all that.

He hadn't been here since the funeral, he realized as he took in his father's large oak desk and high-backed leather office chair. More emotions assaulted him, ones he'd kept at bay for the past nine years.

This was a bad idea. He wasn't ready to face it. He might never be ready, he thought. He missed his father and nine years hadn't changed that. Everything about this room brought back the pain from the Native American rugs on the floor and the two leather club chairs that faced his dad's desk and seat.

He realized he wasn't strong enough for this—maybe especially after being hurt during his last ride and then coming home to find his home was gone. He took one final look and started to close the door. He'd get a motel room for the night rather than show up at a friend's house.

But before he could close the door, his gaze fell on an old Hollywood movie poster on the wall across the room. He felt himself smile, drawn into the office by the cowboy on the horse with a face so much like his own.

He hadn't known his great-grandfather Ransom Del Colt. But he'd grown up on the stories. Ransom had been a famous movie star back in the forties and early fifties when Westerns had been so popular. His grandfather RD Colt Jr. had followed in Ransom's footprints for a while before starting his own Wild West show. RD had traveled the world ropin' and ridin' until late in life.

He moved around the room, looking at all the photographs and posters as if seeing them for the first time. The Colts had a rich history, one to be proud of, his father said. Del Colt, James's father, had broken the mold after being a rodeo cowboy until he was injured so badly that he had to quit.

Del, who'd loved Westerns and mystery movies, had gotten his PI license and opened Colt Investigations. He'd taught his sons to ride before they could walk. He'd never stopped loving rodeo and he'd passed that love on to his sons as if it was embedded deep in their genes.

James limped around the room looking at all the

other posters and framed photographs of his rodeo family. He felt a sense of pride in the men who'd gone before him. And a sense of failure on his own part. He was pushing thirty-six and he had little to show for it except for a lot of broken bones.

Right now, he hurt all over. The bronc he'd ridden two days ago had put him into the fence, reinjuring his leg and cracking some of his ribs. But he'd stayed on the eight seconds and taken home the purse.

Right now he wondered if it was worth it. Still, as he stood in this room, he rebelled at the thought of quitting. He'd made a living doing what he loved. He would heal and go back. Just as he'd always done.

In the meantime, he was dog tired. Too tired to go look for a motel room for the night. At the back of the office he found the bunk where his father would stay on those nights he worked late. There were clean sheets and quilts and a bathroom with a shower and towels. This would work at least for tonight. Tomorrow he'd look for something else.

Lorelei Wilkins pulled into her space in the alley behind her sandwich shop and stared at the pickup parked in the space next to it. It had been years since she'd seen anyone in the building adjoining hers. She'd almost forgotten why she'd driven down here tonight. Often, she came down and worked late to get things ready for the next day.

Tonight, she had brought down a basketful of freshly washed aprons. She could have waited until morning, but she'd been restless and it was a nice night. Who was she kidding? She never put things off for tomorrow.

Getting out, she started to unload the basket when she recognized the truck and felt a start. There were rodeo stickers plastered all over the back window of the cab, but the dead giveaway was the LETRBUCK personalized license plate.

Jimmy D was back in town? But why would he... She recalled hearing something about a fire out on his land. Surely, he wasn't planning to stay here in his father's old office. The narrow two-story building, almost identical to her own, had been empty since Del Colt's death nine years ago. Before that the structure had housed Colt Investigations on the top floor with the ground floor office rented to a party shop that went broke, the owners skipping town.

Lorelei had made an offer on the property, thinking she would try to get a small business in there or expand her sandwich shop. Anything was better than having an empty building next door. Worse, the owners of the party-planning store had left in a hurry, not even bothering to clean up the place, so it was an eyesore.

But the family lawyer had said no one in the family was interested in selling.

As she hauled out her basket of aprons, she could see a light in the second-story window and a shadow moving around up there. Whatever James was doing back in town, he wouldn't be staying long—he never did. Not that she ever saw him. She'd just heard the stories.

Shaking her head, she tucked the basket under one arm, unlocked the door and stepped in. It didn't take long to put the aprons away properly. Basket in hand, she locked up and headed for her SUV.

She couldn't help herself. She glanced up. Was she hoping to see the infamous Jimmy D? Their paths hadn't crossed in years.

The upstairs light was out. She shook her head at her own foolishness.

"Some women always go for the bad boy," her stepmother had joked years ago when they'd been uptown shopping for her senior year of high school. They'd passed Jimmy D in the small mall at the edge of town. He'd winked at Lorelei, making her blush to the roots of her hair. She'd felt Karen's frowning gaze on her. "I just never took you for one of those."

Lorelei had still been protesting on the way home. "I can't stand the sight of Jimmy D," she'd said, only to have her stepmother laugh. "He's arrogant and thinks he's much cuter than he is."

"Don't feel bad. We've all fallen for the wrong man. And he *is* cute and he likes you."

Lorelei had choked on that. "He doesn't like me. He just enjoys making me uncomfortable. He's just plain awful."

"Then I guess it's a good thing you aren't going to the prom with him," Karen said. "Your friend Alfred is obviously the better choice."

Alfred was her geek friend who she competed with for grades.

"Jimmy D isn't going to the prom," she said. "He's too cool for proms. Not that I would go with him if he asked me."

Lorelei still cringed at the memory. Protest too much? Her stepmother had seen right through it. She told herself that all that aside, this might be the perfect opportunity to get him to sell the building to her. But it would mean approaching Jimmy D with an offer knowing he would probably turn her down flat. She groaned. From what she'd heard, he hadn't changed since high school. The only thing the man took seriously was rodeo. And chasing women.

FORMER SHERIFF OTIS OSTERMAN pulled his pickup to the side of the street to stare up at the building. Lorelei Wilkins wasn't the only one surprised to see a light on in the old Colt Investigations building.

For just a moment, he'd thought that Del was still alive, working late as he often did. While making his rounds, Otis had seen him moving around up there working on one of his cases.

The light in that office gave him an eerie feeling as if he'd been transported back in time. That he could rewrite history. But Otis knew that wasn't possible. One look in the rearview mirror at his white hair and wrinkled face and he could see that there was no going back, no changing anything. But it was only when he looked deep into his own eyes—eyes that had seen too much—that he felt the weight of those years and the questionable actions he'd taken.

But like Del Colt, they were buried. He just wanted them to stay that way. Blessedly, he hadn't been reminded of Del for some time now. He'd gone to the funeral nine years ago, stood in the hot sun and watched as the gravedigger covered the man's casket and laid sod on top. He told himself that had been the end of a rivalry he and Del had fought since middle school.

He watched the movement up there in Del's office. It had to be one of Del's sons back from the rodeo. Small towns, he thought. Everyone didn't just know each other. Half the damned town was related.

Otis drove down the block, turning into the alley and cruising slowly past the pickup parked behind Del's narrow two-story office building.

He recognized the truck and swore softly under his breath. Del Colt had left behind a passel of sons who all resembled him, but Jimmy D was the most like Del. Apparently, he was back for a while.

The former sheriff told himself that it didn't necessarily spell trouble as he shifted his truck into gear. As he drove home though, he couldn't shake the bad feeling that the past had been reawakened and it was coming for him.

Chapter Three

James woke to the sun. It streamed in the window of his father's office as he rose and headed for the shower. Being here reminded him of the mornings on his way to school that he would stop by. He often found his father at his desk, already up and working. Del Colt's cases weren't the kind that should have kept his father from sleep, he thought as he got dressed.

They were often small personal problems that people hoped he could help with. But his father treated each as if it was more important than world peace. James had once questioned him about it.

They may seem trivial to you, but believe me, they aren't to the people who are suffering and need answers, Del had said.

Now, showered and dressed, James stepped from the small room at the back and into his father's office. He hesitated for a moment before he pulled out his father's chair and sat down. Leaning back, he surveyed the room and the dusty window that overlooked Main Street.

He found himself smiling, recalling sitting in this chair and wanting to be just like his dad. He felt such

a sense of pride for the man Del had been. His father
had raised them all after their mother's death. James
knew that a lot of people would have said that Del had
let them run wild.

Laughing, he thought that had been somewhat true.
His father gave them free rein to learn by their mistakes.
So, they made a lot of them.

Everything was just as his father had left it, he realized as he looked around. A file from the case his father had been working on was still lying open on his
desk. Next to it were his pen and a yellow lined notepad with Del's neat printing. A coffee cup, the inside
stained dark brown, sat next to the notepad.

A name jumped out at him. Billy Sherman. That kid
who'd been killed in a hit-and-run nine years ago. *That
was the case his father had been working on.*

He felt a chill. The hit-and-run had never been
solved.

A knock at the door startled him. He quickly closed
the case file, feeling as if he'd been caught getting into
things that were none of his business. Private things.

He quickly rose, sending the chair scooting back-
ward. "Yes?"

"Jimmy D?" A woman's voice. Not one he recognized. He hadn't told anyone he was coming back to
town. He'd returned unannounced and under the cover
of darkness. But clearly someone knew he wasn't just
back—but that he was here in Del's office.

He moved to the door and opened it, still feeling as
if he were trespassing. The light in the hallway was
dim. He'd noticed last night that the bulb had burned

out sometime during the past nine years. But enough sunlight streamed in through the dusty window at the end of the hall to cast a little light on the pretty young woman standing before him.

"I hope I didn't catch you at a bad time," she said, glancing past him before settling her gaze on him again. Her eyes were honey brown with dark lashes. Her long chestnut brown hair had been pulled up into a no-nonsense knot that went with the serious expression on her face. She wore slacks, a modest blouse and sensible shoes. She had a briefcase in one hand, her purse in the other. She looked like a woman on a mission and he feared he was the assignment.

LORELEI LOOKED FOR recognition in the cowboy's eyes and seeing none quickly said, "I'm sorry, you probably don't remember me. I'm Lorelei Wilkins. I own the sandwich shop next door." When he still hadn't spoken, she added, "We went to school together?" She realized this was a mistake.

He was still staring at her unnervingly. When he finally spoke, the soft timber of his low voice surprised her. She remembered the unruly classmate who'd sat next to her in English, always cracking jokes and acting up when he wasn't winking at her in the hall between classes. She realized that she'd been expecting the teenaged boy—not the man standing before her.

"Oh, I remember you, Lori," he drawled. "Hall monitor, teacher's assistant, senior class president, valedictorian." He grinned. "Didn't you also read the lunch menu over the intercom?"

She felt her cheeks warm. Yes, she'd done all of that—not that she'd have thought he'd noticed. "It's *Lorelei*," she said, her voice coming out thin. She knew her reputation as the most uptight, serious, not-fun girl in the class.

"I remember that too," he said, his grin broadening.

She cleared her throat and quickly pressed on. "Look, Jimmy D. I saw your light on last night and I—"

"It's James."

"James…?" she repeated. She suddenly felt tongue-tied here facing this rodeo cowboy. Why had she thought talking directly to him was a good idea? She wished she'd tried his family lawyer again instead. Not that that approach had done her any good.

She took a breath and let it out, watching him wince as he shifted his weight onto his obviously injured leg. Seeing that he wasn't in any shape to be making real estate deals, she chickened out. "I just wanted to welcome you to the neighborhood."

"I'm not staying, in case that's what you're worrying about. I mean, not living here, exactly. It's just temporary."

She suspected that most everything about his life was temporary from what she'd heard. She was angry at herself for not saying what she'd really come to say. But from the look on his bruised face and the way he'd winced when he'd shifted weight on his left leg, she'd realized that this wasn't the right time to make an offer on the building. He looked as if he would say no to her without even giving it a second thought.

From her briefcase, she awkwardly withdrew a ten percent off coupon for her sandwich shop.

He took it without looking at it. Instead, his intense scrutiny was on her, making her squirm.

"It's a coupon for ten percent off a sandwich at my shop," she said.

He raised a brow. "Who makes the sandwiches?"

The question was so unexpected that it took her a moment to respond. "I do."

"Huh," he said and folded the coupon in half to stuff it into the pocket of his Western shirt.

What had made her think she could have a professional conversation with this…cowboy? She snapped her briefcase closed and turned to leave.

"Thanks," he called after her.

Just like in high school she could feel his gaze boring into her backside. She ground her teeth as her face flushed hot. Maybe she'd been wrong. Maybe some things never changed no matter how much time had gone by.

JAMES SMILED TO himself as he watched Lorelei disappear down the hall. He hadn't seen her in years. As small as Lonesome was, he'd have thought that their paths would have crossed again before this. But she didn't hang out at Wade's Broken Spur bar or the engine repair shop or the truck stop cafe—all places on the edge of town that he frequented when home. Truth was, he never had reason to venture into downtown Lonesome because he usually stayed only a few days, a week at most.

Seeing Lorelei had made him feel seventeen again.

The woman had always terrified him. She was damned intimidating and always had been. He'd liked that about her. She'd always been so smart, so capable, so impressive. In high school she hadn't seemed to realize just how sexy she was. She'd tried to hide it unlike a lot of the girls. But some things you can't cover up with clothing.

What surprised him as he closed the door behind her was that she still seemed to be unaware of what she did to a man. Especially this man.

He sighed, wondering what Lorelei had really stopped by for. Not to welcome him to the neighborhood or give him a sandwich coupon. It didn't matter. He knew that once he found a place to stay, he'd probably not see her again.

Something bright and shiny caught his eye lying on the floor next to his father's desk. He moved toward it as if under a spell. He felt a jolt as he recognized what it was. Picking up the silver dollar money clip, he stared down, heart pounding. Why hadn't his father had this on him when he was killed? He always carried it. *Always.*

James opened it and let the bills fall to the desktop. Two twenties, a five and three ones. As he started to pick them back up, he noticed that wasn't all that had fallen from the money clip.

He lifted the folded yellow lined notepad paper from the desk. Unfolding it he saw his father's neat printing and a list of names. As was his father's habit, he'd checked off those he had interviewed. But there were six others without checks.

James stared at the list, realizing they were from

Del's last case, seven-year-old Billy Sherman's hit-and-run. His father had stuck the list in his money clip? Had his father been on his way to talk to someone on that list? Why had he left the clip behind? He'd always had so many questions about his father's death. Too many. Ultimately, after what the sheriff had told him, he'd been afraid of the answers.

Moving behind the desk, he sat down again and opened the case file. His father's notes were neatly stacked inside. He checked the notes against the list. Everyone Del had interviewed was there, each name checked off the list.

But the list had stopped with a name that made his jaw drop. Karen Wilkins? Lorelei's stepmother? Why had his father wanted to talk to her? She lived a half dozen blocks from where the hit-and-run had happened.

Chapter Four

James glanced at the time. Almost one in the afternoon. He'd lost track of time reading his father's file on the hit-and-run. Finding Karen Wilkins name on the list had scared him. He couldn't imagine why Del wanted to talk to her.

He'd gone through everything several times, including all of his father's neatly handwritten notes. Del didn't even use a typewriter—let alone a computer. He was old-school through and through.

James realized that after everything he'd gone through, he still had no idea why Karen's name was on the list or why it might be important.

His stomach growled. He thought of the coupon Lori had given him. Pulling it from his pocket, he reached for his Stetson. It was a short walk next door.

As James entered the sandwich shop, a bell jangled over the front door. From the back, he saw Lori look up, her expression one of surprise, then something he couldn't quite read.

He walked up to the sign that said Order Here and scanned the chalkboard menu. His stomach rumbled again.

He couldn't remember when he'd eaten—sometime yesterday at a fast-food place on the road. He'd been anxious to get home only to find he no longer had a home.

Lori appeared in front of him. "See anything you'd like?"

He glanced at her. "Definitely." Then he winked and looked up at the board again. He heard her make a low guttural sound under her breath. "I'll take the special."

She mugged a face. "It comes with jalapeño peppers and a chipotle mayonnaise that you might find too...spicy."

He smiled. "I'm tougher than I look."

She glanced at the leg he was babying and cocked a brow at that.

"It was a really big bronco that put me into the fence. For your information, it didn't knock me off. I held on for the eight seconds and came home with the money."

"Then it was obviously worth it," she said sarcastically. "Let me get you that sandwich. Is this to go?"

"No, I think I'll stay."

She nodded, though he thought reluctantly. When she'd given him the coupon, he could tell that she'd never expected he would actually use it. "If you'd like to have a seat. Want something to drink with that?"

"Sure, whatever's cold." He turned and did his best not to limp as he walked to a table and chair by the front window. This time of the day, the place was empty. He wondered how her business was doing. He wondered also if he'd made a mistake with what he'd ordered and if it would be too spicy to eat. He'd eat it. Even if it killed him.

What was it about her that he couldn't help flirting with her when he was around her? There'd always been something about her... He couldn't imagine how they could be more different. Maybe that's why she'd always made it clear that she wasn't in the least interested in him.

Fortunately, other girls and then women had been, he thought. But as he caught glimpses of her working back in the kitchen, he knew she'd always been an enigma, a puzzle that he couldn't figure out. Flirting with her sure hadn't worked. But, like his father, he'd always loved a good mystery and seldom backed down from a challenge.

Was that why he couldn't let this go? He needed to find out why her stepmother was on Del's list. Why the list was tucked in Del's money clip and why he hadn't had it on him that night. James knew he might never get those answers. Just as he might never know how his father ended up on the train tracks that night. So, what was the point in digging into Del's old unsolved case?

Wouldn't hurt to ask a few questions, he told himself. He wasn't going anywhere for a while until he healed. He had time on his hands with nothing to do—nothing but seeing about getting the wreckage from his burned trailer hauled away and replacing it with a place to live. He told himself he'd get on that tomorrow.

Lori brought out his sandwich and a tall glass of iced lemonade along with plastic cutlery and napkin roll. She placed the meal in front of him and started to step away. He grabbed her hand. She flinched.

"Sorry," he said quickly as he let go. "I was hoping

since you aren't busy with customers that maybe you could sit down for a minute. Join me?"

"I guess I could spare a moment." She hesitated before reluctantly slipping into a chair across from him.

He smiled over at her. "I feel like you and I got off on the wrong foot somehow." He waited for her to say something and realized he could wait all day and that wasn't going to happen. She wasn't going to help him out. He took a sip of the lemonade. "Delicious. Let's start with the truth. What did you really come by for earlier? It wasn't to welcome me to the neighborhood."

She shook her head. "This isn't the time or the place." He raised a brow at that, making her groan. "You never change. Are you like this with every woman?" She raised a hand. "Don't answer that. I already know." She started to get up, but he stopped her.

"Seriously, you can tell me."

She studied him for a long moment before she asked, "Has your family lawyer mentioned that I've made several inquiries about buying your father's building?"

"Family lawyer?"

"Hank Richardson."

"Oh, him." James frowned. "He's our family lawyer? I guess I didn't realize that." She sighed deeply. "Why do you want to buy the building?"

"No one is using it. The place is an eyesore. I might want to expand into it at some point."

He nodded. "Huh. I'll have to give that some thought."

"You do that." She started to rise.

"Wait, I'm serious. I'll think about it. Now can I ask you something else?" She looked both wary and suspicious. "I was going through an old case file of my father's earlier. It was the one he was working on when he died. You might remember the case. Billy Sherman. Killed by a hit-and-run driver. So, I'm looking into it and—"

Her eyes widened. "What are you doing?"

He couldn't help but look confused. "Having lunch?"

"You're not a licensed private investigator."

"No, I'm not pretending to be. I just found the case interesting and since I have some time on my hands..."

She shook her head. "Just like that?" She sighed. "Are you living next door now?"

"For the moment. It's not that bad."

"Like your latest injury isn't that bad?" she asked, clearly upset with him.

"I'll heal, but if you must know my cracked ribs still hurt like hell." He took a tiny bite of his sandwich and felt the heat even though he'd mostly gotten bread. He knew instantly what she'd done. "This is good."

She was watching him as he took another bite. "I make my own bread."

"Really?" The heat of the peppers was so intense that they felt as if they would blow the top of his head off.

"You don't have to sound so surprised."

"Don't take this wrong, but back in high school, I never thought about you in the kitchen baking bread."

"Doubt you thought about me at all," she said and slipped out of her chair.

But as she started past, he said, "I thought about you all the time. But I was smart enough to know you were out of my league."

She'd stopped next to his table and now looked down at him. Her expression softened. "You don't have to eat that. I can make you something else."

He shook his head, picked up his sandwich and took another big bite. He'd eat every ounce even if it killed him, which he thought it might. The intense heat made its way down his throat to his chest. It felt as if his entire body was on fire. He sucked in his breath. Somehow, he managed to get the words out. "This isn't too spicy."

She shook her head. At least she was smiling this time as she walked away.

Chapter Five

James had a lot of time to think since his spicy lunch
had kept him up most of the night. It was a small price
to pay, he told himself. He wasn't sure exactly what he'd
done to Lori in high school or since that had her so upset
with him. He'd been the high school jock and goof-off
who'd gotten by on his charm. She'd been the studious,
hardworking serious student who'd had to work for her
grades. Why wouldn't she resent him?

But he suspected there was more to it than even his
awkward attempts at flirting with her. He felt as if he'd
done something that had made her dislike him. That
could be any number of things. It wasn't like he went
around worrying about who might have been hurt by
his antics back then. Or even now, he admitted honestly.

He kept going over the conversation at lunch though.
She'd tried to pass off her anger as something from high
school. But he wasn't buying it. She hadn't been a fan
of his for apparently some time, but when she'd gotten
upset was when he'd said he was looking into his father's last case, Billy Sherman's hit-and-run.

Add to that, her stepmother's name was on his fa-

ther's list. Del Colt had been meticulous in his investigations. He'd actually been really good at being a PI.
Karen Wilkins wouldn't have been on that list unless
his father thought she knew something about the case.

James was convinced by morning that he needed
to talk to Karen. He knew Lori wasn't going to like it.
Best that he hadn't brought it up at lunch.

But first, he wanted to talk to the person who'd hired
his father to look into the hit-and-run after the police
had given up.

ALICE SHERMAN GASPED, her hand over her heart, her
eyes wide as she stared at James. It seemed to take her a
moment to realize she wasn't looking at a ghost. "For a
moment I thought… You look so much like your father."

James smiled, nodding. "It's a family curse."

She shook her head as she recovered. "Yes, being
that handsome must be a terrible burden for you, especially with the ladies."

"I'm James Colt," he said, introducing himself and
shaking her hand. "I don't think we've ever met." Alice
worked at the local laundry. "I was hoping to ask you
a few questions."

She narrowed her eyes at him. "About what?" She
seemed really not to know.

"I hate to bring it back up and cause you more pain,
but you hired my father to look into Billy's death. He
died before he finished the investigation."

"You're mistaken," she said, fiddling with the collar of her blouse. "I didn't hire your father. My ex did."

That caught him flat-footed. He'd seen several checks

from Alice Sherman in his father's file and Alice had been the first on Del's list of names. He said as much to her.

Her expression soured. "When my ex's checks bounced, I paid Del for his time. But what does that have to do with you?"

"I'm looking into the case."

Alice stared at him. "After all these years? Why would you do that? You...? You're a private investigator?"

"No. It was my father's last case. I'm just looking into it."

"Well, I'm not interested in paying any more money." She started to close the door.

"Please, Mrs. Sherman," he said quickly. "I don't mean to remind you of your loss. I just want to know more about your son."

She managed a sad smile. "Billy is *always* on my mind. The pain never goes away." She opened the door wider. "I suppose I have time for a few questions."

As James took the chair she offered him, she walked to the mantel over the fireplace and took down a framed photograph of her son.

"This is my favorite snapshot of him." She turned and handed it to him. It was of a freckle-faced boy with his two front teeth missing smiling broadly at the camera. "Billy was seven," she said as she took a seat on the edge of the couch facing him. "Just a boy. He was named after my father who died in the war."

"You've had a lot of loss," James said as she brushed a lock of her hair from her face. After the accident, it was as if she'd aged overnight. According to his father's file, Alice would now be forty-five. Her hair was almost entirely gray and there were deep lines around her eyes and mouth. "I'm so sorry. I don't want to make it worse."

"Have you found new information on the case?" she asked, her gaze intent on him. He realized that he might have given her the wrong impression.

"No, not yet. I'm not sure where my father had left the case. Had he talked to you about his investigation before his death?"

"He called me that afternoon, asked if I was going to be home. He thought he might be getting close to finding the hit-and-run driver," she said. "I waited for him but he never showed up. I found out the next day about his pickup being hit by the train."

"He said he thought he might be close to solving the case?" He felt hope at this news. Maybe he wasn't playing at this. Maybe there was something he could find after all. "Did he tell you anything else?"

She shook her head. "Unfortunately, that's all he said."

This news had his heart hammering. He'd always wondered if his father's so-called accident had anything to do with the case. If he was that close to finding the hit-and-run driver... Sheriff Otis Osterman's investigation had ruled Del's death an accident due to human error on his father's part. Either Del hadn't been paying attention and not seen the train coming at the uncontrolled railroad crossing or he'd tried to outrun the train.

Neither had sounded like his father.

The autopsy found alcohol in his father's system and

there had been an empty bottle of whiskey found on the floor of his pickup.

James had never accepted that his father had been drunk and hadn't seen the train coming. If he was close to solving the Billy Sherman case, there is no way he would have been drinking at all.

Alice had gotten up and now brought over more photographs of her son. He'd been small and thin. A shy boy, not an adventurous one. There'd been two theories of how Billy ended up outside on the street that night. The obvious one was that he'd sneaked out for some reason. The other was that he'd been abducted.

"Is there any reason Billy might have left the house that night after you put him to bed?" James asked cautiously.

"No, never. Billy would have never gotten up in the middle of the night and gone out for any reason. He was afraid of the dark. He hated admitting it, but he still slept with a night-light. He was also terrified of storms. There was a terrible storm that night. The wind was howling. Between it and the pouring rain you could hardly see across the street." She shook her head, her gaze unfocused for a moment as if she were reliving it. "He *wouldn't* have gone out on his own under *any* circumstances."

"So, you're still convinced that someone abducted him?"

"His bedroom window was wide open." Her voice broke. "The wind had blown the rain in. His floor and bedding were soaked when I went in the next morning to wake him up and found him gone." All of this he'd already read in his father's file. He could see it was a story she'd told over and over, to the sheriff, to Del, to herself. "I started to call the sheriff when Otis drove up and told me that Billy had been found a few blocks from here lying in the ditch dead." She made angry swipes at her tears. He could see that she was fighting hard not to cry.

"The sheriff said he didn't find any signs of a forced entry," James said. "According to my father's notes, you said you locked the window before tucking Billy in at nine. Maybe you forgot that night—"

"No, I remember locking it because I could see the storm coming. I even closed the blinds. It's no mystery. The only way Billy would leave the house was if his father came to his window that night. Sean Sherman. Not that he'll tell you the truth, but I know he took my boy. Have you talked to him?"

"Not yet." He was still working on the angle that Billy, like every red-blooded, American boy, had sneaked out a time or two. Having been a seven-year-old at one time, he asked, "Did Billy have his own cell phone?" She shook her head. "What about a walkie-talkie?"

"Yes, but—"

"Who had the other two-way radio handset?"

He watched her swallow before she said, "Todd. Todd Crane. But he swore he hadn't talked to Billy that night."

"I'm just covering my bets," James said quickly. He gathered that his father hadn't asked her this. "Did the sheriff talk to Todd?"

"I don't know. I think your father asked me about

Billy's friends, but my son wouldn't have left the house that night even for his best friend, Todd."

James rose to lay a hand over hers as she gripped the stack of framed photos of her son. "Do you mind if I see his room?" Even before she led him down the hall, he knew Billy's room would be exactly like he'd left it even after nine years.

It was a classic boy's room painted a pale blue with a Spiderman bedspread and action figures lined up on the bookshelf.

Moving to the window, James examined the lock. It was an old house, the lock on the window old as well. Maybe Billy *had* been abducted and the sheriff had missed something. But wouldn't there have been footprints in the wet earth outside Billy's window? Unless he'd been taken before the storm hit and the prints had been washed away.

James left, promising to let Alice Sherman know if he discovered anything helpful. The look in her eyes was a stark reminder of what he'd set in motion. He'd gotten her hopes up and the truth was, he had no idea what he was doing.

KAREN WILKINS WASN'T HOME. Her car wasn't parked in front of her freshly painted and landscaped split-level. Nor was it in the garage.

Todd Crane, who would now be around sixteen, hadn't been on his father's list. But Del had talked to Todd's stepmother, Shelby Crane.

Since it was a Saturday, James figured the boy wouldn't be in school. He swung by the house only a few blocks from Alice Sherman's. The woman who answered the door was considerably younger-looking than Alice. Shelby Crane was a slim blonde with hard brown eyes.

"Yes?" The way she was holding the door open only a crack told him that Alice might have already called her.

"I'm James Colt and—"

"I know who you are. What do you want?"

"I'm guessing that you spoke with Alice," he said. "I'd like to talk to your son."

"No." She started to close the door, but he stopped her with his palm.

"Your son might know why Billy Sherman was outside that night," he said, his voice growing harder with each word.

"Well, he doesn't."

"If that's true, then I can't see why he can't tell me that himself."

"He doesn't know. He didn't know nine years ago. He doesn't know now." Again, she started to close the door and again he put a hand on it to stop her.

"Did he and Billy talk on walkie-talkies back then?"

"My son had nothing to do with what happened to that boy. You need to go. Don't make me call the sheriff." She closed the door and this time he let her.

As he started to turn and leave, he saw a boy's face peering out one of the upstairs windows. Then the curtain fell back, and the boy was gone. He wondered why Shelby was so afraid of him talking to her son.

His phone rang as he was getting into his pickup. Melody? He picked up.

"I just got a call from the sheriff's department," she said without preamble. "Carl said you have to get a permit to remove the burned trailer from your land."

"Why would he call you?"

Silence, then a guilty, "I might have tried to hire someone to haul it away before you got back."

James shook his head. Did she not realize he would have noticed anyway? The missing double-wide and the burned area around it would have been a dead give-away. "No problem. I'll swing by and pick up a permit. Thanks for letting me know."

He was still mentally shaking his head when he walked into the sheriff's department.

Sheriff Carl Osterman, younger brother of the former sheriff Otis Osterman, was standing outside his office with a large mug of coffee and the family sour expression on his face. A short stocky man in his late fifties, Carl believed in guilty until proven innocent. Word was that he'd arrest his own grandmother for jay-walking, which could explain why he was divorced and not speaking with his mother or grandmother, James had heard.

"Wondered when I'd be seeing you," the sheriff drawled. "Suppose you heard what happened out at your place."

"It was fairly noticeable."

Carl took a long moment to assess him over the rim of his mug as he slurped his coffee. "You know those meth dealers?"

"Nope. I was on the road. I didn't even know Melody had rented the place."

The sheriff nodded. "You need a permit to haul that mess off."

"That's why I'm here."

"What are you planning to do out there?" Carl asked.

James shook his head. "I don't have any plans at the moment."

"Heard you were staying in your father's old office."

News traveled fast in Lonesome. "My family still owns the building."

Carl nodded again, still eyeballing him with suspicion. "Margaret will give you a form to fill out. Could take a few days, maybe even a week."

"I'm in no hurry."

"That mean you're planning to stay for a while?"

James studied the man. "Why the interest in my itinerary, Carl?"

"There's a rumor circulating that you've reopened your father's office and that you're working one of his cases. Last I heard you weren't a licensed private investigator."

He hid his surprise, realizing that Shelby Crane had probably called. "No law against asking a few questions, but now that you mention it, I worked for my father during high school and when I was home from college and the rodeo so I have some experience."

"You need a year and a half's worth before you can apply for a license under state law."

He pretended he always knew that. "Yep, I know.

Got it covered. Application is in the mail." It wasn't. But damn, he just might apply now.

The sheriff put down his coffee cup with a curse. "Why would you do that unless you planned to stay in town?"

James smiled. He *wasn't* planning to. "Just covering my options, sheriff."

"The state runs a criminal background check, you know."

He laughed. "Why would that concern me?"

"If you have a felony on your record—"

"I don't," he said with more force than he'd intended.

"Good thing they don't check finances or your mental health."

James laughed. "Not worried about either." With a shake of his head, he turned and walked over to Margaret's desk. Without a word, she handed him the permit application.

"You'll need to pay twenty-five dollars when you return that permit," Carl called after him.

OTIS HAD JUST gotten through mowing the small lawn in front of his house. The summer air smelled of cut grass and sunshine. He turned on the sprinklers and, hot, sweaty and tired, went inside. He'd only just opened a can of beer and sat down when Carl called.

"You know what that damned Colt boy has gone and done now?" his brother demanded. James Colt was far from a boy, but Carl didn't give him a chance to reply. "He's been going all over town asking questions about his father's last case. He thinks he's a private eye."

He didn't have to ask what case. Otis was the first one on the scene after getting the call about the boy's body that was found in the ditch next to a house under construction in the new subdivision near where the Shermans lived. The memory still kept him awake some nights. He'd been a month away from retiring. Carl had been his undersheriff. The two of them had worked the case.

"Legally, James can't—"

"He's applied for a state license!" Carl was breathing hard, clearly worked up. "He says his experience working with his father should be enough. It probably is. It's so damned easy to get a PI license in this state, he'll get it and then—"

"And then *nothing*," Otis said. "He's a rodeo cowboy. I heard he's hurt. Once he feels better, he'll be back in the saddle, having put all of this behind him. Even if that isn't the case—which it is—he's inexperienced, the Sherman case is ice cold and we all know how hard those are to solve. And let's face it, he's not his father. I'll bet you five bucks that he quits before the week is out."

Carl sighed. Otis could imagine him pacing the floor of his office. "You think?"

"You know I don't throw money around."

His brother laughed. "No, not Otis Osterman." He sighed again. "I just thought this was behind us."

"It is," he said even though he knew it might never be true. Billy Sherman's death was unsolved, justice hadn't been meted out and what happened that night remained a mystery. There were always those who couldn't live with that.

Unfortunately, Del Colt had been one of them. Him and his damned digging. He'd gotten into things that had been better off left alone.

But Otis had five dollars that said James Colt was nothing like his father. For the young rodeo cowboy's sake, he certainly hoped not.

Chapter Six

After leaving the sheriff's office, James drove aimlessly around town for a while. He knew he should quit right now before he made things any worse. What had he hoped to accomplish with all this, anyway? Was he so arrogant that he thought he could pick up where his father had left off on the case and solve it just like that?

So far all he'd done was stir up a wasp's nest that was more than likely going to get him stung. If he hadn't left Melody in his trailer, if she hadn't rented it, if the renters hadn't blown it up, if he'd gone to a motel and never gone to his father's office...

He reminded himself that getting involved with Melody was all on him. He thought of one of his father's lectures he and his brothers had been forced to endure growing up.

Life is about consequences, Del would say. *Whatever you do, there will be a repercussion. It's the law of nature. Cause and effect.*

What are you trying to say? one of his brothers would demand, usually himself most likely. *'Cause the effect I'm getting is a headache.*

His father would give him a reprimand before adding, *Don't blame someone else when things go wrong because of something stupid you did. Take responsibility and move on. It's called growing up.*

He and his brothers had made fun of that particular lecture, but it had never seemed more appropriate than right now.

His stomach growled. He looked at the time. Two in the afternoon. He hadn't had breakfast or lunch. He drove downtown. There was a spot in front of the sandwich shop. He took that as a sign.

"Tell me you aren't going to make a habit of this," Lori said when he walked in, but she smiled when she said it.

He smiled back at her. Distractedly he studied the chalkboard. The special today was a turkey club. He shifted his gaze to her. "I'll take the special and an iced tea."

"Do you want that on white, wheat or rye?"

"White." He hadn't been *that* distracted that he hadn't noticed her. Today she was dressed in a coral blouse and black slacks. The blouse was V-necked exposing some of the freckled skin of her throat and a small silver heart-shaped locket that played peekaboo when she moved. Her hair was pulled up again, making him wonder if it would fall past her shoulders if he let it down. "With mayo."

"It will be just a few minutes," she said, straightening her blouse collar self-consciously before hurrying into the back.

He took his usual seat. His leg was better today but

his ribs still hurt. He kept thinking about his father's case, wishing he hadn't opened up this can of worms. Now that he had, what choice did he have?

Which meant he would have to talk to Karen Wilkins. Her stepdaughter wouldn't like it. Of that, he was certain. He just hoped that neither was involved. He liked Lorelei. He always had. Her stepmother owned a workout studio in town. Widowed, Karen was active in the community and had been as long as James could remember. He used to think "stepmother like stepdaughter." So why did Del have Karen on his list?

Deep in thought, he started when Lorelei set down the plate with his sandwich in front of him. She gently placed the glass of iced tea, giving him a worried look.

"You all right?" she asked. "You seem a little skittish."

He smiled at that. "I've been better."

"Is it true?"

"That's a wide-open question if I've ever heard one."

"Are you really applying for a private investigator's license?"

He chuckled. Thanks to the sheriff, he was. Probably also thanks to the sheriff everyone in town now knew. "Yep. How do you feel about that?"

She seemed surprised by the question. "It has nothing to do with me."

He nodded, hoping it was true. "Still, you seemed to have an opinion yesterday."

Lori looked away for a moment, licked her lips with the quick dart of her tongue, and said, "I was going to apologize for that."

"Really?" he said as he picked up his sandwich and took a bite. He chewed and swallowed before he said, "And I thought you were going to apologize for trying to kill me with that sandwich you made me yesterday."

Her cheeks flushed. "You didn't have to eat it," she said defensively.

He held her gaze. "Yes, I did."

The bell over the front door jangled. She looked almost relieved as she went to help the couple that came in.

Chapter Seven

After James finished his sandwich and iced tea, he wrote a note on the bill Lori had dropped by on her way past his table. The shop had gotten busy. He could see her through the small window into the kitchen. She was making sandwiches in her all-business way. It made him smile. Whatever she did, she did it with so much purpose.

He wondered what would happen if she ever let her guard down. He wished he could be there when she did.

As he left, he pulled out the list of names. It was time to talk to Karen Wilkins and relieve his mind. She couldn't be involved. He had to find out why she was on the list.

James was surprised how young Karen looked as she opened the door. A small woman with chin-length blond hair and large luminous brown eyes, the aerobics instructor was clearly in great shape. In her late forties, Karen and her stepdaughter could have almost passed for sisters rather than stepmother and stepdaughter.

From the expression on her face though, she wasn't glad to see him. He wondered if it had anything to do with him taking over his father's old case. Or if it was more about his reputation. Would he ever live down his misspent youth?

"I hope I haven't caught you at a bad time," he said. She was dressed in leggings, a T-shirt and sneakers as if on her way to her exercise studio. "Do you have a few minutes? I'd like to ask you a few questions."

The woman chuckled, reminding him of Lorelei for a moment. "Whatever you're selling Jimmy D—"

He raised his hands. "Not selling anything. I've taken over my father's old private investigative business temporarily. I'm looking into the last case he was working on before he died."

She raised an eyebrow and he saw her expression turn both serious—and wary.

"I'm here about Billy Sherman's hit-and-run."

Her eyes widened. "Wasn't that almost ten years ago?"

"It was. Please, I promise not to keep you long."

She didn't move. "Why would you think I would know anything about that?"

"Because you were on my father's list of people he wanted to interview."

Her face paled and he saw the fear. She quickly looked away. "I can't imagine how I could possibly help even if I didn't have a class in a few minutes." Her gaze shifted back to his but only for a second. "I was just leaving. I'm sorry. This really isn't a good time." With that, she closed the door.

He stood for a moment feeling shaken to his core. He knew from experience what guilt looked like. Fear too. Turning, he walked out to his pickup and had just slipped behind the wheel when Karen Wilkins's garage door gaped open, and her car came flying out. She barely missed the front bumper of his pickup before she sped away.

She seemed to be in an awful hurry to get to her class, he thought as he gave it a moment before he followed her.

"WHAT'S WRONG?" LORELEI felt panicked at the fear she heard in her stepmother's voice the moment she'd answered her phone.

"It's...nothing, I'm sorry."

"It's not nothing. I can hear it in your voice. Mom—" Lorelei's mother died when she was three. Both her parents had been young—her mother twenty-two when she died, her father twenty-four. She barely remembered her mother. After her mother died, her father went for ten years before even dating.

It had been a shock when he'd come home from an insurance conference with Karen who had looked like a teenager at twenty-five. Lorelei had been thirteen, Karen only twelve years older. People said they could be sisters. At the time, the comment had made her sick to her stomach. How could her father do this to her?

Lorelei hadn't accepted the woman into their lives for a long time, refusing to call her mom. But at some point, her stepmother had won her over and she'd begun calling her mom since she'd never really had a mother before Karen.

The only time she called her Karen had been when

she was angry at her like for grounding her or mentioning that she had a boyfriend when her father had said she was too young to have one. Most of the time though, she and Karen had been as close as biological mother and daughter.

"I'm just being silly," Karen said now. "I had a little bit of a scare, for no good reason really. Let's forget it. Tell me how you are doing."

Lorelei looked to the ceiling of her shop kitchen. "I'm doing fine. Had a busy lunch crowd and now I'm prepping for tomorrow." Just like she did every day. "Mom, tell me what's wrong. You never call me at work."

"I shouldn't. I know how busy you are."

"I'm not busy right now. Talk to me."

Silence, then finally, "James Colt is back in town. Apparently, he's taking over his father's investigations business?"

"I don't know. Maybe. Mom, why—"

"That boy is trouble. He always has been. I just don't like the idea of him being in the same building as you."

"He's not in the same building," she said, unable to understand why her stepmother was so upset over this. "He's staying next door in his father's office."

"So, you've seen him?"

"He's stopped by for sandwiches a couple of times." She realized that her stepmother was calling from her car. "Are you in your car? Where are you going?"

"Nowhere. I mean…to the store. I'm out of milk."

Her stepmother didn't drink milk. Nor did she hardly eat anything but fruit and vegetables. Her stepdaughter owned a sandwich shop and her stepmother didn't eat even gluten-free bread. "Are you sure you're all right?"

"Sometimes I just need to hear my daughter's voice. I didn't mean to scare you."

Scare her? Lorelei realized that was exactly what she'd done. Scare her. This wasn't like Karen. Whatever had upset her... She realized that it seemed to be James Colt and his plan to take over his father's PI business. It had upset her too, but Lorelei had her reasons going all the way back to middle school. She couldn't imagine first how her stepmother had heard and second why that would upset her unless...

"Mom," she said as a bad feeling settled in her stomach. "Did James come by to see you?"

"I'm at the store about to check out," her stepmother said. "I have to go. Talk to you later." She disconnected.

Lorelei held the phone feeling a wave of shock wash over her. Her stepmother had just lied to her. She wasn't in the store checkout. Karen had still been in her car driving. She'd heard the crunch of tires on gravel. Where had her stepmother gone? Not the store with its paved parking lot.

She quickly called her back. But got voice mail straight away. She didn't leave a message.

AT FIRST KAREN WILKINS seemed to be driving aimlessly around town. James had finally pulled over on a side street with a view of Main Street near her exercise studio and waited. She pulled in front of the studio and he'd thought she was going to get out.

But a few minutes later, she took off again without

getting out of the car. If she'd had a class, someone else was now teaching it apparently. This time, she headed out of town. James waited until another car got behind Karen Wilkins's car before he pulled out and followed.

A few miles out of town, he saw her brake lights come on ahead of him right before she turned down a gravel road and disappeared into the pines. He caught up, turned and followed the dust trail she'd made, wondering if she was finally going to park somewhere.

He didn't have to wonder long. Around a curve in the road, he saw her car stop in front of a large house set back in the pines. Pulling over, he watched her exit her car and hurry up the steps. As she rang the doorbell, she looked around nervously, before the door opened a few moments later.

The man in the doorway quickly pulled Karen Wilkins into his arms, holding her for a moment before he wiped her tears and then kissed her passionately. As he drew her inside, he glanced around—giving James a clear view of his face—before he quickly closed the door.

James felt as if he'd touched a live wire. He let out a low curse. He'd been hoping that he was wrong about Lorelei's stepmother. He'd hoped there was a simple explanation for her being on his father's list. James still didn't want to believe it, but there was no doubt that he'd upset Karen Wilkins on his visit to her house. Since then she'd been running scared.

And look where she'd run. Straight into the arms of Senator Fred Bayard.

Chapter Eight

James drove back into town, stopping in at the local hardware store that his friend Ryan owned. He found him in the back office doing paperwork. "What is Senator Bayard doing in Lonesome?"

His friend looked up and laughed. "You don't get out much, do you? Fred had a summer home built here about ten years ago. He's one of my best customers, always building something out there on his property."

James didn't follow politics. The only reason he'd recognized the man was because his face had been in so many television ads before the last election. "Why here?"

Ryan leaned forward, his elbows on his desk. "His family's from here. It isn't that unusual. What has got you so worked up? I didn't know you were back in town, let alone that you cared about politics."

"Wait, the senator's from Lonesome?" That couldn't have been something he'd missed.

"His mother was Claudia Hanson, the postmistress. Fred grew up here. He was your father's age. Claudia moved them to Helena at some point when she married Charles Bayard, also a senator, and Bayard adopted Fred."

"I never knew that."

"His great-grandfather started the original sawmill here in Lonesome about the time the railroad was coming through. Heard he made a bundle making and selling railroad ties to the Great Northern. Did you pay any attention at all during Montana history class?"

"Apparently not." He vaguely remembered this, but it had been out of context back then. "You've met him then?"

"Fred? He's a good old boy. Like I said, he stops in when he's in town, which isn't often. Most of the time he's in DC. The rest of the time, he's building corrals or barns or adding onto the summer house, even though he spends so little time here during the year."

James sank into the chair across from Ryan's desk, thinking about what he'd just seen. Karen in the man's arms. "Doesn't he have a wife?"

"Mary? I don't think I've ever seen her. She doesn't spend much time here. They have a big place outside of Helena. I think she stays there most of the time doing her own thing. Why the interest?"

He shook his head. "Have you ever seen him with another woman?"

Ryan looked surprised. He leaned back in his chair. "I'm guessing you have. Someone I know?"

"I'm probably mistaken." He quickly changed the subject. "I'm back for a while. I supposed you heard about Melody and my trailer." His friend nodded. "I'm staying at my dad's old office for the time being." He chewed at his cheek for a moment. "I'm thinking about getting my PI license."

"Seriously?"

"I need to heal up before I go back on the rodeo circuit. I thought it would give me something to do."

Ryan narrowed his gaze. "If I didn't know you so well, I might believe that. What's really going on?"

He sighed. "I'm kind of working Del's last case, Billy Sherman's hit-and-run death. It's never been solved."

"Like a tribute to your old man?"

"Maybe."

"And you think Senator Bayard is involved?"

He shook his head. "I was following a lead that made me aware of Bayard. You said he had his summer home built about ten years ago? So, he might have been here at the time of Billy Sherman's accident."

Ryan gave him a wary look. "Where are you going with this?"

James pulled off his Stetson and raked a hand through his hair. "I have no idea. I'm probably just chasing my own tail."

His friend laughed. "I'd be careful if I were you. Bayard carries a lot of weight in this state. Talk is that he might run for governor."

"Don't worry. I'm just following a few leads. I hate that Del didn't get to finish the case." He thought about mentioning what Alice had told him. That Del said he was close to solving it—and was killed that very night.

But he knew what it would sound like and Ryan knew him too well. Conspiracy theory aside, he had his own reasons for fearing what he might find if he dug into his father's death. His father had been acting strangely in those weeks—or was it months—before his death. Something more than the case had been bothering him.

"How's things with you?"

Ryan motioned to the paperwork stacked up on the desk. "Busy as usual. More people are finding Lonesome. I bought the lumberyard a few years ago. Quite a few new houses coming up, so that's good. You thinking about building out there on your place?"

"I'll see what my brothers want to do when they get back after the rodeo season."

"You can't see yourself staying long-term?"

A fleeting image of Lorelei popped into his head, followed by the little girl on the horse. He shook his head. "Nope, can't see myself staying."

LORELEI CLOSED THE shop right after her last customer left. She usually stayed open until six, but tonight she was anxious to leave. She'd tried to call her stepmother numerous times, but each call had gone to voice mail. After how frantic Karen had sounded earlier...

She parked out front. No sign of her stepmother's car. As she started toward the front door, she checked the garage and felt a surge of relief. Her car was parked inside. At the front door she knocked. Normally she just walked right in. But nothing about earlier had felt normal.

"Lorelei?" Her stepmother seemed not just surprised to see her but startled. True, Lorelei hadn't stopped over to the house for a while. She'd been so busy with the sandwich shop. "Is something wrong?"

"How can you ask that?" Lorelei demanded. "You called me earlier clearly upset and when I tried to call you back, my call went straight to voice mail. I've been worried about you all afternoon."

"I'm so sorry. I guess I turned my phone off. Come in." She moved out of the doorway.

As she stepped in, she tried to breathe, admitting to herself just how scared she'd been and how relieved. Her stepmother seemed okay. But Karen wasn't easily rattled. Instead, she'd always taken things in her stride. In fact, she'd seemed really happy for a long while now. Except for the way she'd sounded on the phone earlier.

She turned to study her stepmother and saw something she hadn't before. How had she not noticed the change in her? Karen Wilkins was practically glowing. She was always slim and trim because she often led classes at her studio. But she appeared healthier and happier looking.

"You look so…good," she said, unable to put her finger on what exactly was different about her stepmother.

Karen laughed, brown eyes twinkling, clearly pleased. "Why, thank you."

"Has something changed?"

Her stepmother's smile quickly disappeared, replaced by a frown. "Why would you ask that?"

"I don't know. You just seem…different."

Brushing that off, Karen headed for the kitchen cupboard, saying over her shoulder, "I made some granola. I was going to call you and see if you—"

"Mom. Stop. Why were you so upset earlier when you called me?"

Her stepmother froze for a moment before turning to face her. "I feel so foolish. I got worked up over nothing." Lorelei put her hands on her hips, waiting.

Finally, Karen sighed and said, "James Colt paid me a visit."

Which explained her stepmother's reaction to him staying in the building next to the sandwich shop. "He came here? Why would he—"

"He's taking over one of his father's old cases apparently and was asking questions about something that happened years ago."

Lorelei noticed that her stepmother was twisting the life out of the plastic bag with the granola in it. "What case?"

"That hit-and-run... The boy, Billy Sherman."

"Why would he ask *you* about that?" But she was thinking, why would that upset her stepmother so much?

Her stepmother turned back to the cupboard. Lorelei watched her busy herself with fixing a bag to send home with her. "I have no idea. He's probably asking a lot of people in the neighborhood."

Lorelei frowned. The accident had happened probably a half mile from her stepmother's house. "I'm sure that's all it was," she said, even though her pulse was spiking. She knew her stepmother. Something was definitely wrong. "It still doesn't explain why you were so upset."

Karen sighed. "I was just sorry to find out that he's back in town and in the office next to you given the crush you had on him in high school."

"I didn't have a crush on him in high school!" she protested, no doubt too much.

"Lorelei, I was there. I saw your reaction to that boy. You're doing so well with your business. I'm just afraid you're going to get mixed up with him."

"I'm not getting mixed up with him. He's come over to the shop a couple of times. I don't know where you got the idea I had a crush on him."

Her stepmother merely looked at her impatiently before she said, "Here, take this home." Karen thrust the bag of granola into her hands and looked at her watch. "I'm sorry I have a class I'm teaching this evening. I wish you could stay and we could watch an old movie." She was steering her toward the door. Giving her the bum's rush, as her father would have said.

She wanted to dig her heels in, demand to know why she was acting so strangely. Was it really because she was worried about Lorelei and James Colt, her new neighbor, the cowboy impersonating a PI?

That was ridiculous.

JAMES HAD BEEN at his father's desk, head in his hands, when the pounding at his door made him jump. What the— "Hold your horses!" he called as he rose to go to the door. "What's the big—" He stopped when he saw Lori standing there.

Her face was flushed, her brown eyes wide, her breathing rapid as if she'd run up the stairs. She was still wearing what she'd had on earlier.

"Is there a fire?" A shake of her head. "Are you being chased by zombies?" A dirty look. "Then I give up."

He leaned against the doorjamb to survey her, giving her time to catch her breath. He had a pretty good idea what had her upset, but he wasn't going to bring it up unless she did.

"Why are you questioning my stepmother about the hit-and-run accident?" she demanded.

"Why don't you step in and we can discuss this like—"

"Do you have any idea how much you upset her?"

He nodded slowly. "Actually, I do. Which makes me wonder why, and now why you're even more upset."

Lori took a breath then another one. Her gaze swung away from him for a moment. He watched her regain control of her emotions. She swallowed before she looked at him again. "Why did you question her?" Her voice almost sounded in the normal range.

He moved aside and motioned her into the office. With obvious reluctance, she stepped in, stopping in the middle of the room.

"I love what you've done with the place," she said derisively.

James glanced around, seeing things through her eyes. "I've been meaning to buy a few things to make it more…homey. I've been busy."

"Yes," she said turning to glare at him. "Intimidating my stepmother."

"Is that what she told you?"

A muscle jumped in her jaw. "I will ask you again. Why my stepmother?"

"She was on my father's list."

Lorelei stared at him. "What list?"

He stepped around behind the desk, but didn't sit down. "My father had a method that worked for him. Did you know he solved all of his cases? He was methodical. I wish I was more like him." He could see her growing more impatient. "He would write down a list of names of people connected to the case that he wanted to talk to. He'd check off the ones as he went. Your stepmother was on the list. He hadn't gotten around to questioning her before he was killed. I decided to take up where he left off and ask her myself."

"And?"

"And nothing—she got upset, said she had a class and threw me out."

"Maybe she did have a class."

He gave her a you-really-believe-that look? He watched all the anger seep from her. She looked close to tears, her back no longer ramrod straight, her facial muscles no longer rigid.

"Why would she know anything about Billy Sherman?" she asked quietly.

He shrugged and stepped around the desk to dust off one of the leather club chairs. She moved to it as if sleepwalking and carefully lowered herself down. Behind the desk again, he opened the bottom drawer, took out the bottle of brandy his father kept there and two of the paper cups.

After pouring them each a couple of fingers' worth, he handed her a cup as he took the matching leather chair next to her. He noticed her hand trembled as she took the drink. She was scared. He was afraid she had good reason to be.

He waited until she'd taken a sip of the brandy before he asked, "Can you think of any reason your stepmother would be so upset about talking to me about the case?"

She shook her head, took a gulp and looked over at him. "You can't really think that she is somehow involved." When he didn't speak instantly, she snapped, "James, my stepmother wouldn't hit a child and keep going."

"I'm not saying she did. But she might know who did."

Lori shook her head, drained her paper cup and set it on the edge of his desk as she rose. "You really think she would keep a secret like that?"

"People keep secrets from those they love all the time," he said.

She glared at him. "What is that supposed to mean?"

"Just that she might be covering for someone."

Her eyes flared. "If you tell me that you think she's covering for me—"

He rose, raising both hands in surrender as he did. "I'm not accusing you. I'm just saying…" He met her gaze, surprised at how hard this was. He and Lori had gone through school together and hardly said two words the entire time. It wasn't like that much had changed over the past few days, he told himself even as he knew it had. He liked her. Always had.

"I think your stepmother knows something and that's why she got so upset." He said the words quickly.

Her reaction was just as quick. "My stepmother wouldn't cover for *anyone*. Not for such a horrible crime. You're wrong. She doesn't keep secrets." She started toward the door.

"You might not know your stepmother as well as you think you do." All his instincts told him she didn't.

She reached the door and spun around to face him, anger firing those brown eyes again. "What are you trying to say?"

"That your stepmother might have secrets. Maybe especially from you."

She scoffed at that, and hands on her hips demanded to know what he was talking about.

"After I questioned her about Billy Sherman's death, your stepmother headed for her studio, saying she had to teach a class. But instead of teaching, she drove out of town and into the arms of Senator Fred Bayard."

He saw the answer as the color drained from her face. She hadn't known. "I'm sorry." He mentally kicked himself for the pain in her eyes before she threw open the door and stormed out.

He swore as he heard her leave. How did his father do this? He had no idea, but he suspected Del was a hell of a lot better at it than he'd been so far.

Chapter Nine

For the next few days, James avoided the sandwich shop and Lori. He felt guilty for exposing her stepmother. But he'd hoped that Karen Wilkins might be honest with her stepdaughter. He needed to know what the woman was hiding—other than the senator.

He'd called out-of-town body shops and left messages for them to call if they had a front end–damaged car from hitting something like a deer after the date of Billy Sherman's death. He didn't have much hope, given how much time had passed. He also assumed his father had done the same thing nine years ago without much success.

While he waited to hear back, he mulled over the case as he cleaned up the office and back bedroom. He bought a few things to make the place more comfortable by adding a couch, a couple of end tables, a coffee table, a large rug and some bookshelves for more storage.

For the bedroom, he'd bought a new rug for the hardwood floor and all new towels, rug and shower curtain for the bathroom. He'd even replaced his father's old vacuum with a new one and dusted and washed the windows. By the time he was through with all the hauling and cleaning his leg hurt and his ribs ached worse.

But when he looked around the place, he felt better. He'd also sent in his application for his private investigator license and dropped off his permit at the sheriff's office to have the burned-out trailer removed from the property. Margaret had suggested a company that did that kind of work. After a call to them, he was told the work would be done this week.

James had to admit he was pretty impressed with what he'd accomplished. But he was no closer to finding Billy Sherman's killer. Also, he realized that he missed Lori's sandwiches and the time he spent with her. He'd been hitting the local In-N-Out, but had pretty much gone through the fried food menu over the past few days. He found himself craving the smell of fresh-baked bread—and the sweet scent of Lori.

He just wasn't sure what kind of reception he would get so he decided to do some real work first. After pulling out the list of names, he grabbed his Stetson and headed for the door.

Maybe he'd get a sandwich to go, he thought as he locked and closed the office door behind him. He'd worried about Lori since he'd dropped the bombshell. All she could do was throw him out if she really couldn't stand the sight of him, right?

LORELEI HAD DRIVEN straight to her stepmother's house the evening after James had told her about her stepmother's relationship. She'd seen a light on and movement behind the kitchen curtains. Her stepmother's car was in the driveway, which was odd. She'd slowed and was about to pull in when she saw a second shadow behind the kitchen curtains.

She'd quickly pulled away, feeling like a coward. Why hadn't she confronted her stepmother and whoever was in the house with her? She told herself she needed to be calm before she did. That it would be better if she spoke about this with her stepmother when she was alone.

When she'd run out of excuses, she'd driven home and looked up Senator Bayard online. There were publicity photos of him and his wife, Mary, and their three daughters—all adults, but all younger than Lorelei.

James had to be wrong. He'd misunderstood. Although she couldn't imagine what had made him think that her stepmother would have an affair with a married man—let alone keep it from her only stepdaughter.

She knew that was the part that hurt. She and Karen had been close, hadn't they? And yet, the other night when she'd driven by, her stepmother hadn't been alone. Could have been a neighbor over, but Lorelei knew it wasn't true. The shadows had been close, then moved together as if one before breaking apart and disappearing from view. Her stepmother did have secrets.

The bell over the front door of the sandwich shop jangled and she looked up to see James Colt come in. He was the last person she wanted to see right now. Or ever. Emotions came at her like a squad of fighter jets. Mad, angry, embarrassed, upset, worried, resigned and at the same time her heart beat a little faster at the sight of him.

"Any chance of getting a sandwich to go?" he asked almost sheepishly.

"I suppose," she said, still battling her conflicting emotions.

He glanced from her to the chalkboard. She studied him while he studied it. He was wearing a blue paisley-patterned Western shirt that matched his eyes. She wondered if he'd bought it or if it was purchased by a girlfriend. It was tucked into the waist of his perfectly fitting jeans. One of his prizewinning rodeo buckles rounded out his attire. He shifted on his feet, taking her gaze down his long legs to his boots. New boots? She'd heard him hauling stuff in and out the past few days and knew he'd been shopping.

"I'll take the special on a roll," he said.

After all that, he'd chosen the special? "Iced tea?"

"How about a cola?"

"Fine. Have a seat. I'll bring it to you."

He nodded and met her gaze. "Lori—"

Whatever he planned to say, she didn't want to hear it. Turning on her heel, she hurried into the kitchen to make his sandwich and try to calm her pounding heart. What was it about the man that had her hands shaking? He just made her so…so…so not her usual controlled self.

Lori. No one had ever called her anything but Lorelei. Leave it to James to give her a nickname. Leave it to James to say it in a way that made her feel all soft inside.

JAMES COULDN'T GET a handle on Lorelei's mood. He hated to think what she was putting in his sandwich.

Maybe coming here hadn't been his best idea. But he was hungry, and at least for a few minutes he got to breathe in the smell of freshly baked bread and stretch out his legs.

He didn't have to wait long. When he saw her coming, he started to get up but she waved him back down.

"I thought you'd prefer I take it to go."

She shook her head. "Barbecued pork is hard to eat in your pickup, though I'm sure you've managed it before," she said as she sat down in a chair opposite him.

He wasn't sure the last was a compliment so he simply unwrapped his sandwich and carefully lifted the top piece of bun to see what was inside.

"It's just pulled pork, my fresh coleslaw and house special barbecue sauce," she said, sounding indignant.

"It's your special sauce that I'm worried about," he said.

"It's not too spicy. A tough cowboy like you should be able to handle it." Her gaze challenged him to argue.

He put the sandwich back together and took a bite. "Delicious." He took another bite. He really was starved.

"Do you have to keep sounding surprised that I can make a decent sandwich?" she demanded.

"Sorry, it's just that you're so…so…" He waved a hand in the air, wishing he hadn't opened his mouth.

"So? So what? Uptight? Too good to do simple things?"

He took a bite, chewed and swallowed, stalling. "You're so…sexy." He held up a hand as if expecting a blow. "I know it's a cliché that a sexy woman can't cook. Still…"

"Sexy?" She shook her head and let out an exasperated sigh, but she didn't leave his table. He continued eating. He could see her working through a few things. But when she finally spoke, her words took him by surprise. "I need to know why my stepmother is on your father's list."

He wiped his mouth with a napkin and took a drink of the cola. "I don't know. That's why I went to talk to her."

He could see she was struggling with the next question and decided to help her out. "After she got so upset I followed her. She drove all over town, at one point made a couple of phone calls and then drove out of town. I didn't even know the senator had a house here until he opened the front door."

"Just because she went to his house— Isn't it possible they're just good friends?"

He shook his head. "He took her in his arms and kissed her. It was passionate and she kissed him back. They both seemed nervous, worried that someone was watching and hurriedly closed the door."

"Someone *was* watching," she said under her breath. She looked sick to her stomach.

"I'm sorry to be the one to tell you. I was surprised to see her name on the list. I went there hoping she'd tell me why. It was a shot in the dark. But then when she got so upset before I even had a chance to ask her…"

She nodded. "Refill?" she asked, pointing at his cola.

He shook his head. "You haven't talked to her?"

"I haven't wanted to believe it. I was hoping you were wrong." Her gaze came up to meet his. "I suppose if anyone knows a passionate kiss when he sees one, it would be you though."

He laughed, leaning his elbows on the table to close the distance between them. "You give me a lot more credit than I'm due." She harrumphed at that. "Why do I get the feeling that I did something to you back in grade school or high school or this week and that's why you're so angry with me?"

"You didn't. It's just that I know what kind of man you are."

"Do you?" he asked seriously before shaking his head. "I thought you were smarter than to believe everything you hear. Especially about me." He dropped his voice. "I've kissed a few women. But I'm still waiting to kiss the one who rattles me clear down to the toes of my boots."

She raised a brow. "You've been in town for a few days. I'm sure you have one in your sights already."

"Oh, I do," he said, realizing it was true. He just wondered if he'd ever get the chance to kiss her.

LORELEI CALLED HER stepmother after James left. "I was thinking we could have dinner together tonight if you don't have any plans. I could pick up—" She was going to suggest something vegan for her stepmother, when Karen interrupted her.

"You don't have to pick up anything. I can make us a nice salad for dinner."

She felt off balance. She'd been half expecting her stepmother to make an excuse because she was seeing her…lover again tonight? "Sure, that would be great."

"Good, then I'll see you about six thirty," Karen said.

"See you then."

She disconnected, telling herself that James was wrong. That what she'd seen last night might not even have been the senator. That her stepmother's name being on Del Colt's list meant nothing.

When she arrived at the house a little after six, her stepmother answered the door smiling and seeming excited to see her. She ushered her into the kitchen where she'd made a pitcher of lemonade. "I thought we could eat out on the patio. It's such a beautiful evening."

Lorelei had planned to question her after they ate, but she realized she couldn't sit through chitchat for an hour first. She watched her stepmother start to pour them each a glass of lemonade over ice.

"Are you having an affair with Senator Bayard?"

Her stepmother's arm jerked, lemonade spilling over the breakfast bar. Without looking at her, Karen slowly set down the pitcher, then reached for a dishcloth to clean up the mess. Without a word, she'd already admitted the truth.

"I can't believe this," Lorelei cried. "When did this happen? *How* did this happen? He's *married*!"

Her stepmother turned to her, her face set in stone. "He's getting a divorce and then we're going to get married."

"That's what they all say," she snapped. "Don't you watch daytime talk shows?"

"He's separated and has been for some time. He's been staying at the family's summer home here when he isn't in Washington." Karen looked down at the dishcloth in her hands. "We've been seeing each other for a while now." She looked up.

"Before he and his wife were supposedly separated." It wasn't a question.

"I'm not proud of it. It just happened."

Lorelei shook her head. *"It just happened?"*

"I love him and he loves me."

She bit her tongue, thinking how different this conversation would have been if she'd been the one having the affair. Her stepmother would be hitting the roof right now. Look how upset she'd supposedly gotten over James Colt being in the building next door to her stepdaughter. "You haven't said how you met him."

"Our paths crossed a few times while he was here building his summer home," she said. "We found we had a lot in common."

Lorelei wanted to ask what, but she wasn't ready to hear this. "You're serious." Of course her stepmother was. That glow she'd noticed. Karen was in *love*. That her stepmother would even consider an affair with a married man told her how head over heels she was with this man.

"With him possibly running for governor, the timing isn't good, but we're going to get married once the fallout from his divorce settles."

She couldn't bring herself to say that she wasn't holding her breath and neither should her stepmother. But she was so disappointed and angry right now that she couldn't deal with this. Karen had cautioned her about men since she was thirteen.

"Let me get the salad and we can go out on the deck and—"

"I'm sorry," she said. "I've lost my appetite." With that she turned and started for the door.

"Lorelei, wait."

She stopped at the door, closing her eyes as she heard her stepmother come up behind her. She thought of all the tantrums she'd thrown as a teen, all the arguments she and Karen had had over the years. They'd always made up and gotten through it.

"I'm sorry I've disappointed you."

"I am too, Karen." She started to open the door, felt her stepmother tentatively touch her back and flinched.

Her stepmother quickly removed her hand. "Disappointed in me or not you have to understand, I'm an adult. I get to make my own decisions, right or wrong." Her voice broke. "I'm still young. I've been lonely since your father died. Can't you try to be happy for me?"

Lorelei felt herself weaken, her love for her stepmother a constant in her life. Karen was right. She was still young and she'd been a widow for years now. Of course she was lonely; of course she wanted a man in her life.

"I'm trying," she said and turned to face her. "Tell me you aren't involved in what happened to the Sherman boy. Swear it on my life."

Her stepmother looked shocked. "Why would you ask—"

"Because I know you. For you to get so upset over James's questions about the case that you'd run to your lover and be seen, you must have something else to hide. Tell me the truth."

Her stepmother took a step back. "So, it was James who saw us and ran right to you to tell you. I should have known."

"He didn't run right to me. I cornered him, demanding to know why he would question you. But you still haven't answered my question," Lorelei said, that knot in her chest tightening. "Swear. On my life."

"Don't be ridiculous," Karen snapped and took another step back. "I would never swear to anything on your life. You're upset and don't know what you're saying. You should go before either of us says something we'll regret."

Lorelei felt tears burn her eyes. "You already have." With that, she opened the door and left.

Chapter Ten

After leaving the sandwich shop, James had felt at loose ends. He drove out to his family's ranch. *Ranch* was a loosely used term since no one had raised much of anything on the land. It was close to a hundred acres covered with pines. Some of it was mountainous while a strip of it bordered the river.

He and his brothers had talked about selling some of it off since they didn't use it, but Willie, their eldest brother, talked them out of it.

"Land doesn't have to do anything and someday you're going to be glad that it's there and that it's ours," Willie had said.

The remains of the double-wide trailer had been removed leaving a scorched area of ground where it had been. But James could see where grass was already starting to grow. It wouldn't be long before nature healed the spot.

James stood looking at the rolling hillsides, towering pines and granite bluffs. He was glad Willie had talked them out of selling even a portion of it. This land was all that brought them back here. It was the one constant

in their lives. The one tangible in their otherwise no-
madic lives.

That and the office building. He thought about Lori
wanting to buy it. He still thought of the place as Del's
and felt himself balk at the idea of ever giving it up.

Back at the office, he found several notes tacked to
his back door. Word had gotten out that he was in business. One was from an insurance company offering him
surveillance work if he was interested. The other was
from someone who wanted her boyfriend followed. He
laughed, delighted that he had several new PI jobs if
he wanted them.

But first he had to finish what he'd started. He drove
out to Edgar Appleton's house some miles from town.
Edgar owned a heavy equipment construction company. He and his crew had been working near where
Billy Sherman's body had been found. One of his em-
ployees, Lyle Harris, had been operating a front loader
that morning. He was about to dump a load of dirt into
the ditch when a neighbor woman spotted the body and
screamed—stopping him.

Edgar lived on a twenty-acre tract. His house sat off
to one side, his equipment taking up the rest of the property. Several vehicles were parked in front of the house
when James climbed the steps to knock. He could hear
loud voices inside and knocked again.

A hush came from inside the house a moment before
the door opened. Edgar filled the doorway. He was a big
man with a wild head of brown hair that stuck up every
which way. He was wearing a sweatshirt with his busi-

ness logo on it and a pair of canvas pants. It appeared he'd just gotten home from work.

"If this is a bad time..."

"James Colt," Edgar said in a loud boisterous voice. "Bad time? It's always a bad time at this house. Come in!" He stepped aside. "Irene, put another plate on the table."

She yelled something back that he didn't catch just a moment before she appeared behind her husband wiping her hands on her apron. "You'd think I'm only here to cook and clean for this man." She smiled, her whole face lighting up. "Get on in here. I have a beef roast and vegetables coming out of the oven. I hope your table manners are better than Ed's. I could use some stimulating conversation for once." Her laugh filled the large room as she headed back to the kitchen.

"The meanest woman who ever lived," Edgar said so she could hear it. Her response was swift, followed by the banging of pots and pans. "I don't know what I would do without her."

"That's for sure!" she called from the kitchen.

"I can't stay for dinner. I probably should have called first," James said.

"Sorry, but you have no choice now," Edgar said as he looped an arm around his shoulders and dragged him in. "She'll swear I ran you off and I'll have to hear about it the rest of the night."

He had to admit, Irene's dinner smelled wonderful. He heard his stomach growl. So did Edgar. The man laughed heartily as he swept him into the dining room off the kitchen.

"I didn't come for dinner, but it sure smells good," he told Irene as she brought out a pan of homemade rolls. "Let me help you with that." He grabbed the hot pads on the counter and helped her get the huge pot out of the oven. It was enough food to feed an army, he saw. "Are there other people coming?" he asked as she directed him to a trivet at the head of the large dining room table.

"At this house, you never know," Irene said. "I like to be prepared. As it is, Ed didn't bring home half the crew tonight so I'm glad you showed up."

"Me too," Ed said as he sat down at the head of the table and began to slice up the roast. Irene swatted him with the dishtowel she took from her shoulder before she sat to his right and motioned James into the chair across from her.

"James, I want to hear it all," she said smiling as she reached for his plate and Edgar began to load it up with thick slices of the beef. "You know what I'm talking about," she said, seeing his confusion. "Is it true? You've taken over your father's private investigative business? We'll get to Melody and what happened to your trailer later."

"Sorry, I should have warned you," Edgar said with a laugh. "The woman is relentless." As he said it, he reached over and squeezed her arm.

For the rest of the meal, they all talked and laughed. James couldn't recall a time he'd enjoyed more. Seeing how these two genuinely cared about each other was heartwarming and Irene's dinner was amazing.

"I know you didn't come by for dinner," Edgar said when they'd finished and Irene got up to clear the table.

James started to rise to help her but she waved him back down.

He explained that he was looking into his father's last case, the hit-and-run that killed Billy Sherman.

"We were working in that subdivision. You know Lyle, my front-end loader operator, was working that morning," Edgar said. "He was getting ready to fill in that ditch we'd dug when a neighbor lady came over with some turnovers she'd made for the crew. She saw Billy lying there and started screaming." He shook his head. "It wrecked us all." Irene came from the kitchen to place her hand on the big man's shoulder for a few moments before taking the rest of the dirty plates into the kitchen.

"That was a new neighborhood nine years ago, new pavement," James said. "Did you see skid marks, any indication that whoever hit him had tried to stop?"

Edgar wagged his big head. "The sheriff, that was Otis back then, said the driver must have thought he hit a deer and that was why he didn't stop. Plus it was raining hard that night. I reckon the car was going so fast when it hit the boy—he was pretty scrawny for his age—that the driver hadn't known what was hit."

"But the driver had to have known it wasn't a deer, even if he didn't stop," James said. "There would have been some damage to the car, a dent or a broken head-light." Edgar nodded. "I would think the car would have had to have been repaired."

"You're assuming the driver was local, but even if that was the case, he wouldn't have had it repaired in town."

James thought of the next name on his list that his father hadn't gotten to: Gus Hughes of Hughes Body Shop in town. But Edgar was right. If it had been a local, then the driver would have gotten the car repaired out of town.

Irene came in and changed the subject as she served coffee and raspberry pie with a scoop of ice cream.

"I can't tell you how much I've enjoyed this meal," James told her before Edgar walked him to the door.

"I hope you find out who killed that boy," the big man said, patting him on the shoulder. "It's time he was put to rest."

LORELEI WOKE FEELING exhausted after a night of tossing and turning. She kept thinking about her stepmother and going from angry to sad to worried and regretful for the things she'd said. Her stepmother couldn't know anything about Billy Sherman's death. So why hadn't she sworn that? Why had she gotten even more upset and basically thrown Lorelei out of her house?

After a shower, she dressed for work. Owning her own business meant she went to work whether she felt like it or not. She had a couple of women she hired during the busiest seasons to help out, but she'd never considered turning the place over to one of them before this morning.

She reeled her thoughts back. What had she been doing nine years ago when Billy Sherman died? Working in a friend's sandwich shop in Billings, learning the business. Before that she'd had numerous jobs using her college business degree, but hadn't found anything that called to her. She'd always known that she wanted the independence of having her own business.

And what had her stepmother been doing nine years ago? Karen had her exercise studio and had been teaching a lot, as far as Lorelei could remember.

Frowning now, she tried to remember if it had been her stepmother who'd told her about Billy Sherman's hit-and-run or if she'd heard it on the news. Didn't she remember a phone conversation about it? Her stepmother being understandably upset since it had happened not that far from her house in that new adjoining subdivision.

Lorelei felt sick to her stomach and more scared than she'd ever been. She had to know the truth. But if she couldn't get her stepmother to tell her...

It was still early. She called her friend Anita and asked her if she wanted to fill in today, apologizing for the short notice. Anita jumped at the opportunity, saying she had nothing planned and could use the money.

"I had already made a list of the specials," Lorelei told her. "Everything you need is in the cooler. You just have to get the bread going right away. I'll be in to help as soon as I can."

Anita said she was already on her way out the door headed for the shop, making Lorelei smile. Her business would be fine. Grabbing her purse, she headed for her car.

WITH THE RISING SUN, James had awakened knowing he was going to have to talk to former sheriff Otis Osterman at some point. He had too many questions about how the sheriff had handled the investigation. According to his father's notes, Otis had refused to give him any information. James suspected it was one reason his father had taken a case that had still been active.

Del hadn't gotten along with the former sheriff and James had a history with Otis due to his wayward youth. So, he wasn't expecting the conversation was going to go well.

After getting ready for his day, he decided he would talk to Gus Hughes first, then swing by Otis's place out by the river. His father had already talked to Gus, but James thought it wouldn't hurt to talk to him again.

However, when he went downstairs to where his pickup was parked out back of the office building, he found Lorelei Wilkins leaning against his truck waiting for him.

He braced himself as he tried to read her mood. "Mornin'," he said, stopping a few safe feet from her.

She looked as if she didn't want to be there any more than he did. For a moment, he thought she would simply storm off without a word. "I want to hire you."

Of all the things that he'd thought might happen, this wasn't one of them. "I beg your pardon?"

"You heard me," she snapped, lifting her chin defiantly. "What do you charge?"

Good question. He had no idea. Legally, he wasn't a private investigator yet. The application and money had been sent in. He was waiting for his license. "If we're going to talk money, we should at least go somewhere besides an alley. Have you had breakfast?"

"I couldn't eat a thing right now."

"Could you watch me eat? Because I'm starved!" He gave her a sheepish grin. Even after that meal he'd had last night, he was hungry. He figured she might relax more in a public place. She also might not go off on him in a local cafe filled with people they both probably knew.

Because, he suspected before this was over, she would want to tell him what she thought of him.

LORELEI ADMITTED THIS was a mistake as she watched James put away a plate of hotcakes.

"You sure you don't want a bite?" he asked between a forkful.

"I'm sure." The smell of bacon and pancakes had made her stomach growl, reminding her that she hadn't eaten dinner last night. But she still couldn't swallow a bite right now, she told herself. She just wanted to get this over with.

"So, are you going to do it or not?" she demanded.

He finished the hotcakes, put down his fork and pushed the plate aside. She watched him wipe his mouth and hands on his napkin before he said, "What exactly is it you want me to do?"

"I just told you," she said between gritted teeth. Leaning forward and dropping her voice even though there wasn't anyone sitting near them in the cafe, she said, "Find out the truth about my…" She mouthed, "Stepmother."

He seemed to give that some thought for a moment before he said, "Wouldn't the simplest, fastest approach be for you to ask her yourself?"

"I already tried that," she said and sighed.

"And she denied any knowledge?"

She looked away under the intenseness of those blue eyes of his. "Not exactly. She asked me to leave her house."

"Come on," James said, tossing money on the table before rising. "Let's go."

It wasn't until they were in his pickup that he said, "What is it you think I can do that you can't?"

"I thought you had some…talent for this."

"Like what? Throw my magic lariat around her so she tells the truth? Or use my brawn to beat the truth out of her?"

She mugged a face at him. "Of course not. I thought maybe you could break into her house and look for evidence."

Now they were finally getting somewhere, James thought. He disregarded the illegal breaking and entering part and asked, "What kind of evidence?"

She swallowed before she said, "A diary maybe. She used to keep one. Or…maybe a bill from like, say a… body shop for car repairs."

"What would make you think I'd find something like that even if nine years hadn't passed?"

"Because," she snapped, clearly losing patience with him. "If she was the one who hit Billy, then she would have had to have her car repaired, right? Has this thought really not crossed your mind?"

"My father already talked to Gus Hughes at his body shop."

She waved a hand through the air in obvious frustration. "Are you just pretending to be this dense? She wouldn't have taken it to the local body shop. She's smarter than that. She would have taken it out of town. It's not like she could keep it hidden in her garage for long."

"But she also couldn't simply drive it out of town either without someone noticing," he said.

"Maybe she did it at night."

He shook his head. "Still too risky. And how does she explain no car for as long as it was in the body shop?"

"It was summer. She always rides her bike to work in the summer. There must be some way she could get the car out of town to a body shop and get it brought back without anyone being the wiser."

"I have a couple of thoughts on the matter. In fact, I'm talking to someone on my list today about just that. I've already made inquiries of a half dozen body shops within a hundred-mile radius."

She sat back, looking surprised. "So, you *have* thought about all of this?" He didn't answer, simply looked at her. She let out a breath and seemed to relax a little. "You still haven't told me what you charge."

"Let's see what I turn up first, okay?"

Lorelei nodded and looked uncomfortable. "I'm starved. Would you mind stopping at a drive-thru on the way back to your office?"

He chuckled and started the engine. Out of the corner of his eye he watched her. She was scared, and maybe with good reason, that her stepmother was somehow involved.

He'd wanted to solve this case for his father. Also to prove something to himself. But right now he wanted to find evidence to clear Karen Wilkins more than anything else because of her stepdaughter. He wanted to put that beautiful smile back on Lori's face, even as he feared he was about to do just the opposite.

Chapter Eleven

After James dropped Lori off at her shop, telling her he'd think about what she'd asked him to do, he drove out to the river. It was one of those clear blue Montana summer days so he decided to quit putting it off and talk to former sheriff Otis Osterman. He'd save Gus Hughes for later, when he'd be glad to see a friendly face.

He put his window down and let the warm air rush in as he drove. He could smell the pines and the river and sweet scent of new grass. It reminded him of the days he and his brothers used to skip school in the spring and go fishing down by the river. One of his favorite memories was lying in the cool grass, listening to the murmur of the river while he watched clouds drift through the great expanse of sky overhead. His brothers always caught enough fish for dinner that he could just daydream.

The former sheriff lived alone in a cabin at the edge of the water. Otis's wife had died of cancer a year before he retired. He'd sold their place in town and moved out here into this two-room log cabin. His pickup was parked in the drive as James knocked. He knocked louder, and getting no response walked around to the back where he found the man sitting on his deck overlooking the river.

"Hello!" he called as he approached the stairs to the deck. He didn't see a gun handy, but that didn't mean that there wasn't one.

Otis jumped, his boots coming down loudly on the deck flooring.

"Didn't mean to startle you," James said as he climbed the steps and pulled up a wooden stool to sit on since there was only one chair and Otis was in it.

"Too early for company," the former sheriff growled, clearly either not happy to be startled so early—or equally unhappy to see a member of the Colt family anytime of the day.

"I'm not company," he said. "I'm here to ask you about Billy Sherman's hit-and-run."

Otis gave him a withering glare. "Why would I tell you anything?" As if his brother Carl hadn't already told him.

"My father was working the case when he died. I've decided to finish it for him."

"Is that right? You know anything about investigating?"

"I worked with Del from the time I was little. I might have picked up a few things."

Otis shook his head. "You always were an arrogant little bastard."

"That aside, I'm sure you must have had a suspect or two that you questioned."

"Would have come out to your place and talked to

you and your brothers but you felons were all too far away at some rodeo or other to have done it."

"Technically, none of us are felons," James said. "What about damage to the vehicle that hit him? You must have tried to find it."

"Of course we tried. Look, we did our best with what we had to work with. Your father thought he could do better. But he didn't find the person, did he?"

"He died before he could."

"To keep his record intact."

James shook his head. He'd known this would be ugly. "My father didn't kill himself."

"You really think his pickup stalled on the tracks with a train coming and he didn't have time to get out and run?" Otis shook his head. "Unless there was some reason he couldn't get out." He mimed lifting an invisible bottle to his lips.

Bristling, James warned himself to keep the temperature down. If things got out of control, Otis would have his brother lock him up behind bars before he could snap his fingers. "Del did have a shot of blackberry brandy on occasion, but according to the coroner's report, he wasn't drunk."

"But he could have been trying to get drunk after the argument he had with a mystery woman earlier that day in town," Otis said. "At least, that's the story I heard. The two were really going at it, your father clearly furious with her."

James pushed off the stool to loom over the man. "If anyone started that lie, it was you to discredit my father. The only reason he would have taken an open case like

Billy Sherman's was if he thought you and your brother were covering something up. If he hadn't died, what are the chances that he would have exposed the corruption in your department?"

"I'd be careful making wild accusations," Otis warned.

"Why?" He leaned closer, seeing that he'd hit a nerve. "It's never stopped you."

Otis held up his hands. "You've got your grandfather Colt's temper, son. It could get you into a whole pack of trouble."

James breathed hard for a moment before he took a step back. That was one of the problems of living in small-town Montana. Everyone didn't just know your business, they knew your whole damned family history.

"I'm going to find out the truth about Billy Sherman's death. And while I'm at it, I'm going to look into my father's death as well. You make me wonder if they aren't connected—just not in the way you want me to believe."

"You're wasting your time barking up that particular tree, but it's not like you have anything pressing to do, is it? You should be looking for the mystery woman."

James smiled. Otis's forehead was covered with a sheen of sweat and his face was flushed. "You would love to send me on a wild goose chase. Are you that worried that I might uncover the truth about how you and your brother handled the Sherman case? You're wondering if I'm as smart as my father. I'm not. But maybe I'll get lucky."

"Get off my property before I have you arrested for trespassing."

"I'm leaving. But if I'm right, I'll be back, only next time it will be with the real law—not your baby brother."

LORELEI COULDN'T BELIEVE what she'd done. Now that she was away from James, she regretted hiring him and planned to fire him as soon as she saw him. The man didn't even have a private investigator's license. What had she been thinking? He was worse than an amateur. He thought he was more trained at this than he was because he'd run a few errands and done some filing for his father.

It had been a spur-of-the-moment stupid decision and not like her at all. She usually thought things through. She blamed James for coming back and turning her life and her upside down.

Worse, as the day stretched on, she'd also had no luck reaching her stepmother. By almost closing time, she'd already sent Anita home and was prepping for the next day, angry with herself. Not even rock and roll music blasting in her kitchen could improve her mood.

She felt so ineffectual. Had she really suggested to James that he break into her stepmother's house and search for incriminating evidence against her? She groaned at the thought that he might have already done it.

If she really believed he would find such evidence, then why didn't she simply look herself? She had an extra key to the house and she knew when her step-mother should be at the studio.

But she also knew the answer. She was afraid she *would* find something damning and do what? Destroy it?

The front doorbell jangled. She looked up to see the very pregnant Melody Simpson waddle in. "Hey," the young woman called. "Am I too late to get a sandwich?"

She hurriedly turned down the music as she realized she'd forgotten to lock the front door. This was exactly the kind of behavior that was so unlike her.

"Not if you want it to go," Lorelei said, even though she was technically closed.

"Sure." Melody waddled up and studied the board. "White bread, American cheese, mustard and no let-tuce."

Lorelei nodded. "Twelve inch?" A nod. "Anything to drink? I have canned soda to go."

The young woman shook her head and stepped to the closest table to sit down. "My feet are killing me."

Not knowing how to answer that, Lorelei hurried in the back to make her a cheese sandwich. It felt strange seeing James's pregnant former girlfriend. Not that they had dated long before he'd left town. Still...

"I heard about you and Jimmy D," Melody called back into the kitchen.

"Pardon?"

"Breakfast at the cafe this morning early, whisper-ing with your heads together. The two of you were the talk of the town before noon."

Lorelei gasped as she realized the rumors that would

be circulating. She groaned inwardly. Because it had been so early, people might think that she and James had spent the night together!

That thought rattled her more than she wanted to admit. She could just imagine Gladys's Beauty Emporium all atwitter. The place was rumor mill central. She started to tell Melody that it wasn't what it looked like, but the explanation of her early morning meeting with James was worse.

"I just wanted you to know that I'm not jealous," Melody added.

That stopped Lorelei for a moment. Melody wasn't jealous? Why would she be jealous? She finished wrapping up the sandwich, bagged it and went back out front to find the woman had kicked off her shoes and was rubbing her stocking-covered feet.

She put the bag on the counter along with the bill. After a minute, Melody worked her shoes back on and limped over to her. As she dug a wad of crumpled bills from her jacket pocket, Lorelei said, "Why would you be jealous? I heard you were marrying Tyler Grange and having…" Her gaze went to Melody's very distinct baby bump. "His baby."

Melody continued to smooth out singles on the countertop, her head bent over them with undue attention.

Lorelei felt a start. *It was Tyler's baby, right?* "Have your plans changed?" she asked, finding herself counting the months by the size of Melody's belly. What if it was James's? And why did that make her heart plummet?

"Naw, my plans haven't changed. Tyler's going to

marry me," Melody finally said as she finished. Lorelei realized Melody had been counting the bills. She took the fistful of ones. "It's just that I really cared about James. I want him to be happy. I guess if you can make him happy…" She sounded doubtful about that.

"Sorry, but it isn't like that between me and James."

Melody picked up the sack with her sandwich inside. "If you say so. Just don't hurt him. He's real vulnerable right now." With that, she turned and left.

Lorelei followed her to the door and locked it behind her. James vulnerable? That was a laugh. But as she headed back to finish up in the kitchen, she wondered why Melody would even think that.

Shaking her head, she tried to clear James Colt out of it. She hadn't seen him since this morning. She'd checked a few times to see if his pickup was parked out back. It hadn't been. She could have tried calling him—if she'd had his cell phone number.

She told herself she'd fire him when she saw him. She just hoped he hadn't done anything on her behalf and, at the same time wishing he had, but only if he hadn't found anything incriminating.

"Sounds like you had quite the day," Ryan said when James stopped by the hardware store. "I can't believe that you threatened Otis. Wish I'd seen that."

They were in the back office, Ryan's boots up on the desk as he sipped a can of beer from the six-pack James had brought. After his visit with Otis, James had driven around trying to calm down. He'd stopped at a convenience store, picked up the beer and headed for Ryan.

The two of them had roomed and rodeoed together in college. Ryan always knew he would come back and run his father's hardware store. James hadn't given a thought to what he would do after he quit rodeo.

"You'd better watch your back," Ryan was saying. "Otis hates you and his brother is even less fond of you."

"I'm not afraid of that old fart or his little brother." He took a drink of his beer. "I'd love to nail Otis's hide to the side of his cabin."

"I wouldn't even jaywalk if I were you until you leave town again. You know how tight he is with his younger brother. What all did Otis say that has you so worked up?" his friend asked.

James chewed at his cheek for a moment. "He insinuated Del killed himself possibly over a broken heart because of a mystery woman or because he couldn't solve the Billy Sherman case or because he was a drunk and couldn't get out of his pickup before the train hit him."

Ryan raised a brow. "What woman?"

"According to Otis, my father was seen arguing with a mystery woman earlier in the day before he was killed. Apparently not someone from around here since Otis didn't have a name."

"Seriously?"

"He was more than serious. He suggested I should find that woman. It was obvious that he's worried what I might find digging around in the Sherman case—

and my father's death. I'm just wondering why he's so worried."

His friend took a long drink and was silent for a few minutes. "I've always wondered about your old man's accident."

"Me too. What was Del doing out on that railroad track in that part of the county at that time of the night? There are no warning arms that come down at that site. But the lights would have been flashing…" He shook his head. "I've always thought it was suspicious but even more so since I found out that Del told someone that he was close to solving Billy Sherman's case."

Ryan let out a low whistle. "Now you're a private investigator almost, investigate."

He smiled. "Just that simple?"

"Why not? Sounds like it's something you've thought about. Why not set your mind at ease one way or another?"

"Just between you and me? This is a lot harder than I thought. But you're right. I've already got half the town upset with me. Why not the other half?" He looked at his phone and, seeing the time, groaned. "I'd planned on stopping by Gus Hughes's garage. If I'm right, someone had to pay to get their car fixed out of town nine years ago."

"You're thinking it might have been Terry," his friend said. Terry Durham worked for Gus. "Now that you mention it, Terry bought that half acre outside of town a little over nine years ago and put a camper on it. Could be a coincidence. Not sure how much he would charge to cover up a hit-and-run murder vehicle. But since he's usually broke…"

James drained his beer, arced the can for a clean shot at the trash in the corner and rose to leave. "Thanks. I think I'll stop by his place and have a little talk with him."

"Thanks for the beer. Best take these with you." Ryan held up the other four cans still attached to the plastic collars.

James shook his head. "I figure you'll need them if the rumors are true. Are you really dating the notorious Shawna Collins?"

Ryan swore as he hurled his empty beer can at him.

James ducked, laughing. "And you're warning *me* to be careful." He stepped out in the hall before his friend found something more dangerous to throw at him.

Although Del Colt had talked to Terry Durham according to his list—and checked him off—James wanted to ask him where the money had come for his land and trailer.

Terry lived outside of town on a half-acre lot with a trailer on it. James pulled into the woods, his headlights catching the shine of a bumper. In the large yard light, he recognized Terry's easily recognizable car and parked behind it. The souped-up coupe had been stripped down to a primer coat for as long as James could remember seeing it around town.

Getting out of the pickup, he started toward the camper. But stopped at the sight of something parked deep in the pines. A lowboy trailer. The kind a person could haul a car on.

The lowboy trailer was exactly what he wanted to

talk to the man about and he felt a jolt of excitement. Maybe he could solve this.

Whoever had hit Billy Sherman would have had some damage to their vehicle or at the very least would have wanted to get the car out of town and detailed to make sure there was no evidence on it. One way to get the car out of town was on the lowboy. Terry Durham always seemed to need money. Add to that his proven disregard for the law and the huge chip on his shoulder, and you had someone who would look the other way— if the price were right.

Moving toward the camper again, he saw that there appeared to be one small light behind the blinds at the back. He knocked on the door. No answer. No movement inside. Was it possible Terry had come home and left with someone else?

James was debating coming back early tomorrow when he started past Terry's car and caught a scent he recognized though the open driver's side window.

He stopped cold, his guts tightening inside him as he glanced over inside the car.

Terry was slumped down in his seat behind the wheel, his eyes open, his insides leaking out between his fingers.

Chapter Twelve

It was daylight by the time James had told the sheriff his story a dozen times before losing his temper. "I've told you repeatedly, I went out there to talk to Terry about a car he might have been paid to haul to another town."

"Whose car?" Sheriff Carl Osterman asked again.

James sighed. "Billy Sherman's killer whose name I don't know yet."

"You're back in town for a few days and now we have a murder. As I recall, you and Terry never got along. I recall a fistfight my brother had to break up out at the Broken Spur a couple years ago."

"That was between Terry and my brother Davey. I had nothing against Terry and I certainly had no reason to kill him. So, either believe me or arrest me because I'm going home!"

When the sheriff didn't move, James pushed out of the chair he'd been sitting in for hours and headed for the door.

"Don't leave town!" Carl called after him.

He held his tongue as he strode out of the sheriff's department to take his first breath of fresh air. It was morning, the sun already cresting the mountains. He felt exhausted and still sick over what he'd seen earlier.

After he'd called 911 and the sheriff had arrived, he'd been ordered to wait in the back of Carl's patrol SUV while an ambulance was called along with crime techs. Eventually Terry Durham's body had been extricated from the car and hauled off in a body bag.

Even now, it took him a moment to get his legs under him. The last time he'd seen anything like that had been when a bull rider had been gored. He still felt sick to his stomach as he made his way to his pickup. He tried not to think about it. He'd wanted to ask Terry if someone paid him to take their damaged car out of town on that lowboy trailer of his nine years ago.

He'd been hoping the answer wasn't going to be Karen Wilkins. Terry wouldn't have done it for just anyone—unless the price was right.

Now he was dead. James feared it was because of the questions he'd been asking about Billy Sherman's death.

As he pulled up behind the office building, he saw that Lorelei's SUV was already parked behind her shop. He got out and was almost to his door, when she rushed out.

"I need to talk to you," she said. She smelled like yeast, her apron dusted with flour. There was a dusting of flour on her nose. He couldn't imagine her looking more beautiful.

But right now, he just needed some rest. He held up his hands. "Whatever it is, can we please discuss it later." He opened his back door and started to step in when she grabbed his arm.

"Are you sick or drunk?" she demanded.

He turned to look at her. She sounded like the sheriff because he'd had beer on his breath earlier. "I'm not drunk, all right? Lorelei, it's just not a good time. Whatever it is, I'm sure it can wait until I get some sleep."

"Rough night?" she mocked.

"You could say that."

Her gaze suddenly widened. "Oh, no. You found something. You went to my stepmother's and—"

He sighed, realizing why she'd been waiting for him to return. "I didn't go to your stepmother's." She'd hear about this soon anyway. "I went out to Terry Durham's and found him…murdered. I've been at the cop shop ever since."

She let go of his arm. "I'm sorry."

He nodded. "Now I just need a shot of brandy and a little sleep. I've spent hours answering the sheriff's questions. I can't take any more right now." She nodded and stepped back. "Later. I promise. We'll talk then." He stepped through his door, letting it slam behind him as he slowly mounted the stairs.

It wasn't until he reached the office door that he saw the note nailed to it.

Tearing it off, he glanced at the scrawled writing.

Get out of town while you still can.

Inside the office, he unlocked his father's bottom drawer and pulled out the .45 he would be carrying from now on.

LORELEI STARTED AT the sound of her phone ringing. She pulled a tray of bread from the oven and dug her cell out of her apron pocket. "Hello?"

"I hope I didn't wake you." It was her stepmother.

"No. I'm at work. I've been here for hours."

"You must be expecting a big day." Her stepmother sounded almost cheerful.

Right, a big day, she thought remembering her encounter with James not long after sunrise. If that was any indication of how this day was going to go...

"I saw that you called yesterday," her stepmother said when Lorelei hadn't commented. "Sweetheart, I'm sorry about the way we left things. I had to get away for a while." With her lover? Lorelei didn't want to know. "I think we should get together this evening and talk. I'll make dinner. I thought you could come over after work." Her stepmother sounded tentative. "Please, Lorelei. You're my daughter. I love you."

She felt herself weaken. "Fine. But I need you to be honest with me."

"I am being honest with you. I don't know why seeing James upset me, but it had nothing to with Billy Sherman." A lie, she thought. "I was just worried that you were getting involved with him." Another lie? "He's all wrong for you." Yet another lie?

Lorelei closed her eyes to the sudden tears. "I'll see you this evening." She disconnected, hating this. They used to be so close. She feared everything had changed. Her stepmother had hidden a married lover. But that might not be the worst of it.

As she went back to work, she remembered what James had told her. Terry Durham had been murdered. She couldn't remember the last murder in Lonesome—then with a start, realized it would have been Billy

Sherman's hit-and-run. James said he'd found Terry's body. He'd been so upset. Because he felt he might have caused it by asking questions around town from his father's list of people like her stepmother?

She felt a chill even in the warm kitchen. What if the two murders were connected? Hadn't she heard something about Terry getting beaten up after he tried to cheat during a poker game in Billings? But what if Terry was murdered because he worked at the local body shop and knew who killed Billy Sherman?

The thought shook her to her core. What if Billy Sherman's killer had felt forced to kill again? At the sound of a trash can lid banging in the alley, she quickly moved to the back door to look out in time to see James.

When she'd seen him coming in disheveled and exhausted she'd jumped to the conclusion that he'd been out on the town with a woman. It was reasonable given his reputation, but still she felt bad about how quickly she'd judged him. She'd been so ready to add this onto her list of reasons she couldn't trust the man. With a curse, she realized he'd probably thought she'd been jealous.

"Did you get some sleep?" she asked from the doorway.

"Some. Sorry I was short with you earlier."

She shook her head as if it had been nothing. As he joined her, she caught the scent of soap and noticed that his hair was still wet from his shower. He smelled good, something she wished she hadn't noticed. His wet dark hair was black as a raven's wing in the sunlight. It curled at the nape of his neck, inviting her fingers to bury themselves in it, something else she wished she hadn't noticed.

"You wanted to talk to me?"

"You look like you could use a cup of coffee," she said, stalling. "I have a pot on. Interested?"

He hesitated but only a moment. "Sure." He followed her into the kitchen at the back and leaned against the counter, watching her. She could feel the intensity of his gaze on her. She felt all thumbs.

Fire him. Just do it. Like ripping off a Band-Aid. Thank him and then that will be it. You can pretend that you were never so serious as to do something so stupid as hire him to investigate your own stepmother in the first place.

When she turned, he was grinning at her in that lazy way he had, amusement glinting in the vast blue of his gaze. His long legs were stretched out practically to the center of the kitchen as he nonchalantly leaned against her counter. "You want me to help you?"

She thought he meant the coffee and started to say that she had it covered.

"You aren't going to hurt my feelings," he said. "I figured you've changed your mind about hiring me. I don't blame you. Sometimes it's better not to know. And when it's your own stepmother—"

She bristled. "I didn't say I don't want to know if she's involved."

One dark eyebrow arched up. "So, what is it you're having such a hard time saying to me?" he asked as he pushed off the counter and reached her in two long-legged strides.

Lorelei swallowed the lump that had risen in her throat. The scent of soap and maleness seemed to overpower even the aroma of the coffee. Suddenly the kitchen felt too small and cramped. Too intimate.

She stepped around him to the cupboard where she kept the large mugs, opened the door and took down two. Her hands were shaking. "I didn't say I was going to fire you."

"No?" He was right behind her. She could practically feel his warm breath on the back of her neck.

She quickly moved past him with the mugs and went over by the coffee pot.

She heard him chuckle behind her.

"Do I make you nervous?" he asked as she filled both mugs shakily. When she turned around, he was back on the other side of the kitchen, leaning against the counter again, grinning. "I do make you nervous." He laughed. "What is it you're afraid I'm going to do? Or are you afraid I'm *not* going do it?"

"Sometimes you just talk gibberish," she snapped.

His grin broadened. "I want to know when you're going to do what I'm paying you to do."

"Paying me?"

She stepped toward him, shoved one mug full of coffee at him and waited impatiently for him to take it. She wished she'd never suggested coffee. The less time she spent around this impossible man the better. Right now, she wanted him out of her kitchen.

Seeing that he had no intention of going anywhere, she said, "We can talk in the dining room." With that she turned and exited the kitchen, her head up, chin out and her heart pounding. She told herself with every step that she hated this arrogant man. Why hadn't she fired him?

She slipped into a chair, cupping the mug in her hands, her attention on the steam rising from the hot coffee.

He slid into a chair opposite her and turned serious. "Let's face it, Lori. You don't want to know about your stepmother. So let's just forget it and—"

She reached into her pocket, pulled out the key and slapped it down on the Formica table. "That opens the back door to her house."

He stared at the key for a moment before he raised his gaze to her again. "You don't have to do this." She merely stared back, challenging him at the same time she feared she would change her mind. "Fine." He picked up the key and put it in his jeans pocket. Then he took a sip of his coffee.

"What does Terry Durham have to do with Billy's hit-and-run?" she asked.

He looked up in surprise. "I didn't say—"

"You didn't have to." She had a bad feeling that Terry's death had nothing to do with a poker game gone wrong.

"He works at the body shop. As you pointed out yourself, the vehicle that hit Billy would have some damage to it. How would you get it fixed without anyone being the wiser? Get it out of town quickly. Terry had a car-hauling trailer and now he's dead. Add to that, after the hit-and-run, Terry bought a piece of property and a small camper." James shrugged. "It's all conjecture at this point, but it stacks up. I start asking questions and now he's dead."

"What is it you'll look for at my stepmother's?"

"The person who owned the damaged car might have left a trail. Either a receipt from the body shop that fixed it. Or a lump sum withdrawal from a bank account to pay Terry off. But that's if they kept a record from nine years ago."

Her heart pounded. "Give me the key back."

He hesitated only a moment before he dug it out of his jeans and handed it over. "So, I'm fired."

Lorelei shook her head as she pocketed the key again. "No, I'm going with you." He started to put up an argument, but she cut him off. "It will be faster if I go. I know where she keeps her receipts, and her bank account records. Karen keeps everything. Come on," she said, pushing away her unfinished coffee. "She'll be at her studio now."

"You sure about this?" he asked.

"Not at all, but I can't do this alone and I have to know."

He met her gaze. "If what we find incriminates her, I won't cover it up even to protect you."

"You come with integrity?"

"It costs extra," he said to lighten the mood for a moment. "But seriously, if you want to change your mind, now's the time, Lori."

She didn't correct him. In fact, she was getting to where she liked her nickname, especially on his lips. "I'm serious too." She knew she couldn't live with the suspicion. "I have to know the truth before tonight. I'm having dinner at her house."

"Great," he said under his breath as he downed his coffee and rose from the table as she called a friend to come watch the shop.

Chapter Thirteen

James parked in the alley behind the house after circling the block. Karen Wilkins's car wasn't in the drive. Nor had there been any lights on in the house. He could feel Lorelei's anxiety.

He was about to suggest she stay in his pickup, when she opened her door and climbed out. Her expression was resigned. He could tell that she was doing this come hell or high water. She looked back at him, narrowing her eyes and he was smart enough not to argue.

Lori produced the key as they walked through the backyard. The sky overhead was robin egg blue and cloudless, the air already warming with the summer sun. A meadowlark sang a short refrain before they reached the back door.

He watched her take a breath as she unlocked the back door and they stepped in. "Does she keep an office here?"

With a nod, Lori led the way. The office was a spare bedroom with multipurpose use. There was a sewing machine and table and containers of fabric on one side.

A bed in the middle and a small desk with a standing file cabinet next to it.

James headed for the filing cabinet only to find it locked. He looked at Lori who still hadn't spoken. He suspected she was having all kinds of misgivings about this but was too stubborn to stop it.

She opened the desk drawer and dug around for a few moments before she picked up a tiny wooden box that had been carved out of teak.

"My father gave her this." She opened the lid and with trembling fingers removed a tiny key and handed it to him.

He unlocked the top drawer and thumbed through the folders. Then he tried the second drawer. Karen's bank was still sending back the canceled checks nine years ago. He dug deeper and found small check boxes all labeled. She was certainly organized. He looked for personal checks from nine years ago, found the box, handed it to Lori. She sat down at the desk and began to go through them.

"You're looking for a check to Terry Durham or a towing company after Billy Sherman's hit-and-run so after April 10th," James said. "Also, a check to a body shop in another town." She nodded and set to work.

He found Karen's monthly account statement in the third drawer and quickly began to sort through them looking for a large withdrawal after April 10 from nine years ago. He'd just found what he was looking for when he heard a car door slam.

They both froze. "I thought you said she was working," he whispered.

"She was supposed to be. Maybe it isn't her."

James heard a key in the front door lock. "It's her." He grabbed the months he needed of the checking account documents and carefully closed the file drawer. He saw Lorelei pocket a handful of checks and slip the box into the top drawer as he motioned toward the closet.

He opened the door as quietly as possible. It sounded as if Karen had gone to one of the bedrooms on the other side of the house. The closet was full of fabric and craft supplies. There was just enough room for the two of them if they squished together. He eased the closet door closed as the sound of footfalls headed in their direction.

A moment later Karen came into the room. He heard her stop as if she'd forgotten what she'd come in for. Or as if she sensed something amiss? He tried to remember if they had left anything out that could give them away. He didn't think so. But if she opened the desk drawer she would see the check box. As neat and organized as she was, she would know.

He held his breath. He could feel Lori, her body spooned into his, doing the same. Her hair smelled like a spring rain. He could feel the heat of her, the hard and soft places fitting into some of his. He tried to think about baseball.

With relief, he heard Karen leave the room. The front door slammed and he finally let out the breath he'd been holding. A few moments later, a car engine started up. James waited until the sound died away before he carefully opened the closet door.

Lori stepped out, straightening her clothing, looking flushed.

"Sorry about that," he said, his voice sounding hoarse. She pretended she didn't know what he was talking about, which was fine with him. "Let's finish and get out of here."

He went through the bank statements and then Karen's retirement papers. That's when he found it. A large withdrawal of ten thousand dollars.

"Lori?" He realized that she hadn't moved for a moment. She was staring down at a canceled check in her hand. All the color had drained from her face. "What is it?" Without a word, she handed him the check.

The check had been made out to the bank for ten thousand dollars. He flipped it over and saw that the money had been deposited into Lori's account. "I don't understand."

"Nine years ago I looked into getting a loan to open a sandwich shop," she said, her voice breaking. "The bank turned me down. My stepmother had offered to cosign on the loan but I didn't want her risking it if I failed. I had no experience."

"And then you did get the loan," he said.

She nodded. "The president of the bank called, said he noticed I had applied for the loan and that he knew me and was willing to take a chance on me. He lied. It was all my stepmother."

She looked as if she might burst into tears at any moment as she put the check back in the box and opened the file cabinet to put the box away. He watched her relock the file cabinet and put the key back where she'd found it and close the desk drawer.

"I can imagine what you're feeling right now," he finally said.

"Can you?" She turned to face him. "I didn't trust my stepmother. I hired you and then I sneaked in here with you looking for dirt on her. Did we find anything? No. Instead, I find out that she took money out of her retirement to help me open my sandwich shop, the woman I've been at odds with for days because of you."

He didn't feel that was fair, but was smart enough not to say so. "I'm sorry. But we didn't find anything." Instead, he'd found a large withdrawal from a retirement plan but not to cover a crime. "No checks to Terry Durham or a body shop." He held up his hands. "So good news."

She merely glared at him before she pushed past him and headed out the back door. He double-checked the room to make sure they hadn't left anything behind and followed. By the time he reached the pickup, she was nowhere to be seen.

He climbed behind the wheel and waited for a few minutes, but realized his first thought was probably the right one. She'd rather walk back than ride with him. He started the engine and drove out of the alley.

Another great day as a private investigator, he thought with disgust.

CORA SWORE SHE had a sixth sense these days. She'd been in the living room knitting while she watched her favorite television drama when she had an odd feeling. Putting aside her knitting and pausing her show, she went into the kitchen and picked up her binoculars.

These special night vision binoculars had paid for themselves the first night she got them. It truly was amazing what a person could see especially since she lived on a rise over the river.

First she scanned the river road. Only one car parked out there tonight and she recognized it. The same couple that often parked out there on a weekday night. She thought for a moment, wondering if there was any way she could benefit from this knowledge and deciding not, scanned farther downriver.

Tonight not even a bunch of teenagers were drunk around a beer keg. Slow night, she thought, wondering why she'd thought something was going on.

Out of habit, she turned the binoculars on the Colt place. At first she didn't see anything since she wasn't really expecting to—until she saw a pickup coming through the woods on the Colt property with no headlights on. Had she heard the driver pull in? Or did she really have a sixth sense for this sort of thing?

She wondered as she watched the pickup stop on the spot where the burned-out trailer had once stood. James Colt? She waited for the driver to exit the rig. Western hat and a definite swagger, she thought, but she couldn't see the face because he kept his head down.

Following him with the binoculars, she watched as he went around to the back of his pickup and took out a box. It must have been heavy because he seemed to strain under the weight. To her surprise, he carried the box over to where the debris from the burned-out double-wide had been. He hesitated, then put down the box before going back to the pickup. He returned with a small shovel.

She watched, transfixed as he began to dig a hole into which he dumped whatever was in the box. Then he shoveled the blackened earth over the hole.

Shoving back his hat to wipe a forearm across his brow, Cora got her first good look at his face. She felt a start as she recognized him.

Her hand began to sweat because suddenly she was holding the binoculars so tightly, her heart racing in her chest. She watched former sheriff Otis Osterman carry his shovel and the empty box back to the pickup. A moment later he drove off.

LORELEI FELT ASHAMED and guilty and not just because of her stepmother. She'd blamed James for all this when she'd been the one who'd hired him. How could she possibly think her stepmother was involved in Billy Sherman's death? Worse, that her stepmother would try to cover it up? She hated too that she'd felt a wave of relief when they hadn't found anything incriminating. Had she been that worried that they would? She was a horrible stepdaughter. She promised herself that she would make it up to Karen.

The walk back to the shop helped. Fortunately, the moment she entered her kitchen, she had work to do. Anita had a lot done, but there was still more bread to be made before she opened at 11:00 a.m. She thanked Anita, paid her and sent her on home, needing work more today than ever.

When she'd come in the back way, she'd been thankful that James's pickup wasn't anywhere around. She recalled the two of them in the closet, her body pressed into his, and felt her face flush hot as she remembered his obvious…desire. Fortunately, he hadn't been able to feel her reaction to it. At least she hoped not.

"Lorelei?"

She spun around in surprise to see Karen standing in the kitchen doorway. She really needed to start locking the back door.

"Are you all right? You're flushed," her stepmother said as she quickly stepped to her, putting a hand on Lorelei's forehead.

"I'm baking bread and it's hot in here."

Her stepmother looked skeptical but let it go. "I hope you don't mind me stopping by."

She wiped her hands on her apron. "I'm glad you did."

"I know you're busy but I didn't want to do this over the phone. I'm afraid I have to cancel our plans for dinner tonight. I'm sorry. Something's come up."

Lorelei raised a brow, sick to the pit of her stomach at how quickly her suspicions had come racing back. "I hope it's nothing bad."

"No." Her stepmother looked away. "Just a prior engagement I completely forgot about." Lorelei nodded. "So, we'll reschedule in a few days." Karen let out a nervous laugh. "You and I are so busy."

"Aren't we though," she said, hoping the remark didn't come out as sarcastic as it felt. Her stepmother wasn't acting like herself. It wasn't Lorelei's imagination. She wanted to throw her arms around her and hug her although she couldn't thank her for the personal loan without telling her that she'd gone through her checks.

But at the same time, she wanted to demand her stepmother tell her the truth about what was going on. No matter what, she couldn't keep lying to herself. Something was definitely going on with her stepmother besides the affair.

"I'll call you." Her stepmother headed out of the kitchen.

"Mom!" Lorelei's voice broke. "Be careful."

Karen looked surprised for a moment. "You too, dear."

JAMES FELT AS if he'd been spinning his wheels. He knew no more about Billy Sherman's death than he had when he started this. Now he'd alienated someone he had been growing quite fond of since his return to town.

As he was passing a house in the older section of town, he recognized the senior gentleman working in his yard. James pulled up in front of the neat two-story Craftsman with its wide white front porch. Getting out, he walked toward the man.

Dr. Milton Stanley looked up, a pair of hedge clippers in his hands. His thick white eyebrows raised slightly under small dark eyes. "You're a Colt."

He nodded. "James."

"You look like your father."

"My father's why I stopped when I saw you. Could we talk for a minute? I don't want to keep you from your work."

"I was ready for a break anyway." Milton laid down

his clippers, took off his gardening gloves and motioned toward the house. "Take a seat on the porch. I'll get us something to drink."

James followed the man as far as the porch and waited. He could hear the doctor inside the house. Opening and closing the refrigerator. The clink of glass against glass. The sound of ice cubes rattling.

A few minutes later, the screen door swung open with a creak and Milton reappeared. He handed James a tall glass of iced lemonade and motioned to two of the white-painted wooden rockers. Each had a bright-colored cushion. James could imagine the doctor and his wife sitting out here often—before her death.

They sat. James sipped his lemonade, complimented it and asked, "You were coroner when my father was killed. I need to know if you ran tests to see if he was impaired."

The doctor drained half of his lemonade before setting down the glass on one of the coasters on the small round end table between them. James watched him wipe his damp hands on his khaki pants.

Milton frowned. "Why are you asking this?"

"Because of the case he was working on at the time of his death. It was ruled an accident by the sheriff, but I've since learned some things that make me think he might have been murdered."

"Murdered?"

"I'm not sure how, but I've only been working my father's old case a few days and already someone I wanted to talk to has been killed," James said. "I've always questioned my father's death but never more so than now. I've learned that he was close to solving Billy Sherman's hit-and-run."

The doctor frowned. "There was no alcohol or drugs in your father's system at the time of his death."

James blinked, swamped with a wave of relief. "None?"

"None."

The relief though only lasted a moment. "Then how did it happen?" Why didn't he get out of the pickup before the train hit him? Surely, he saw the flashing lights. Did he think he could beat the train? That wasn't like his father. Del was deliberate. He didn't take chances.

Milton shook his head. "Any number of things could have led to it. He might have had something on his mind and didn't notice the flashing lights. The train hit him on the driver's side. He might not have had time to get out. The pickup engine could have stalled. He could have panicked. You can't see that train because of the curve until it's almost on top of you. Your father's accident wasn't the first one at that spot. The railroad really needs to put in crossing arms." He picked up his lemonade and drained the rest of it.

James drank his and placed the empty glass on a coaster on the table. He could tell the doctor was anxious to get back to his gardening. "Thank you for your help."

"I'm not sure I was much help," Milton said and followed him as far as the yard. The doctor picked up his clippers and went back to work.

CORA STEWED. HER favorite television drama couldn't even take her mind off what she'd seen. She tried to work it out in her mind. That was the problem. She wasn't even sure what she'd seen—just that Otis Osterman hadn't wanted to be caught doing whatever it was. Of that she was sure.

Putting her knitting aside again, she picked up her cell phone and muted the television. She let the number ring until she got voice mail. Then she called back. It took four times, one right after the other, before the former sheriff finally picked up.

"What the hell do you want, Cora?" he demanded.

"I bought myself one of those video recorders."

"What?"

"I was trying to learn how to use it and I accidentally videoed the darnedest thing. *You.* You're right there on my video."

"What. Are. You. Talking. About?"

"I couldn't figure out why you would be on the Colt property, let alone why you would dump a box of something into the ashes where the Colt's burned-out trailer had been, let alone why you would then cover it up with that little shovel you keep in your pickup."

She listened to him breathing hard and knew that she'd struck pay dirt. "I'm thinking James Colt would be interested in seeing my little video. Heck, I suspect he'd pay good money given how he feels about you. Trespassing and so much more. So how much do you think my video is worth? Maybe I should just take it to the FBI."

Otis swore and Cora smiled. She could tell by the low growl on the other end of the line that she had him. She didn't care what he'd planted on Colt property. It was no skin off her nose. But she could certainly use a little supplemental income.

"You addled old woman. I don't know what you think you saw—"

"That's why I'm having this young person I met put the video up on the internet. Technology is really something these days. I bet someone has a theory about what you were doing, don't you? Even your brother the sheriff won't be able to sweep this under the rug—not after I make sure everyone knows the man in the video is a former sheriff. That should make it go viral, whatever that is. My new young friend assures me it's good though."

"Maybe I should come out to your place and we should discuss this," Otis said through what sounded like clenched teeth.

"I wouldn't suggest that. I get jumpy at night and you know I keep my shotgun handy. I'd feel terrible if I shot you."

"What do you want?" he demanded angrily.

"Five thousand dollars."

Otis let out a string of curses. "I don't have that kind of money."

"Well, not *on* you. You'll have to go to the bank and when you do, you tell them you borrowed money from me and want to pay it back. Just have them put it into my account. It's a small town. They'll do it. As soon as I get confirmation, I'll drop the video by your cabin. Maybe you'll have something cold for us to drink."

He growled again. "How do I know you won't make copies and demand more money?"

"Shame on you, Otis. They do say crooks are often

the most suspicious people. I wouldn't have a clue how to make a copy."

"I want the camera too."

"Well, now that's just rude. I'm still learning how to use it. But I'll bring it when I bring the video. We can discuss it. With that night vision thing, the camera won't be cheap. Tomorrow then. Have the bank call me. Look forward to seeing you, Otis." She laughed. "In person. I've already seen enough of you in the movies." She laughed harder and disconnected.

Then she went to check her shotgun to make sure it was loaded, putting extra shells in her pocket, before she locked and bolted all the doors.

Chapter Fourteen

When James returned to the office, he saw that it appeared someone was waiting for him. A bike leaned against his building in the alley with a young boy of about sixteen sitting on a milk crate next to it.

As he got out of his truck, the boy rose looking nervous. "Can I help you?" James asked.

"Are you the PI?"

He smiled. "I guess I am."

"I need to talk to you." He looked around to make sure there wasn't anyone else around. "It's about Billy."

In that instant, he realized who this boy must be. "Todd?" The boy nodded. "Does your mom know you're here?" The boy shook his head. "I'm not really supposed to talk to you without a parent present." Then again, he wasn't a licensed PI yet, was he?

"But I'll tell you what," he said quickly seeing the boy's disappointment. The kid had been waiting patiently. He couldn't turn him away especially when Todd might have valuable information. He glanced at the time. "What if we have another adult present who can advise you?"

Todd looked worried. "Who?"

"Hungry?" He asked the boy, remembering himself at that age. His father used to ask if he had a hollow wooden leg. Where else was all that food going?

Todd nodded but then hesitated. "What about my bike?"

"It's safe there." James pushed open the back door into the sandwich shop. Once that smell of fresh bread hit the kid there was no more hesitation.

LORELEI SAW JAMES first and started to tell him he was the last person she wanted to see—when she spotted the boy with him. Her gaze went from the boy to James in question.

"This is Todd. He's hungry." James turned to the kid. "What kind of sandwich would you like?"

"I suppose you don't have a hot dog?" the boy asked her sheepishly.

"Let me see what I can do. Would you like some lemonade with that?" The boy nodded and actually smiled. Her gaze rose to James.

He shook his head since he didn't have a clue what was going on. "We'll just have a seat. We're hoping you can join us. Todd wants to have a talk with us."

"With *us*?"

"You're going to be the adult in the group," James said.

She smirked. "I always am."

He smiled. "I knew I'd picked the right woman for the job. Mind if I go ahead and lock the front door while we talk so we aren't interrupted?" He didn't wait but went to the door and put up the closed sign and locked the door.

She did mind, even though it was past closing time. What was this man getting her into? She made Todd a mild sausage sandwich with a side of ketchup and mustard and poured three lemonades before bringing them out on a tray to the table. She put Todd's in front of him.

"So, what's this about?" she asked as she slid into the booth next to the boy. Todd had already bitten into his sandwich. He gave her a thumbs-up as he chewed.

"Todd was waiting for me behind my office. He wanted to talk to the PI." She raised a brow. "I explained to him that we probably shouldn't talk without an adult present. It's kind of a gray area."

Lorelei shook her head. "I'm not sure I want to be part of this."

"I have to tell him about Billy," Todd said, putting down his half-eaten sandwich. He took a drink of lemonade. "I know what my mom told you when you came over to see her. She forgot that I did have Billy's other walkie-talkie headset that night and that after that, she threw it away."

"You and Billy talked on the two-way radios the night he died?"

Todd nodded, looking solemn.

"About what time was that?" James asked.

"He woke me up. The electricity had gone off but I looked at my Spiderman watch. It was almost ten thirty. I told him not to do it."

James shot her a look before shifting his gaze back to the boy. "Do what?"

"He said he had to go out. That he'd seen someone walk by his house in the rain and that he needed to follow whoever it was."

"His mom told me that Billy didn't like storms," James said, "Why would he go out and follow someone?"

He picked up his sandwich, took a large bite and chewed for a moment before swallowing. "Billy and I had this game we played. We pretended we were spies. We used to pick someone to follow. It was fun. They usually heard us behind them and chased us off. But sometimes we could follow them a really long way before they did."

"Who was he following that night?" James asked.

Todd shook his head. "He said he had to see what they were doing before he chickened out. I told him not to. He said the person was headed down the street in my direction and that I should watch for him and come out. I watched from the window, but I never saw him and then I fell asleep. I just figured he chickened out, like he said. Or his mom made him go to bed and quit using the walkie-talkies."

"How did you pick the people you followed?" James asked.

The boy shrugged. "Sometimes we would just see someone who looked dangerous."

"Dangerous?" Lorelei repeated.

"Sometimes we just wondered where they were going, so we followed them."

"So, Billy just saw someone out the window and decided to go out into the storm to follow them?" she asked, unable to hide her incredulity.

"I guess. It might have been someone he'd been following before that."

"Was it a man or a woman?" Lorelei asked.

"Billy said, 'I just saw someone outside my window. I have to follow and find out what they're doing.' He sounded…scared." The boy looked down at his almost empty plate. "When I heard you asking my mom about Billy, I knew I had to tell you." He bit into what was left of his sandwich and went to work on it.

"Does your mom know about the call from Billy?"

The boy shook his head adamantly. "Billy and I took a blood oath not to ever tell our parents about our spy operations. But I think she was worried that I told Billy to go out that night and that everyone would blame me. I didn't. I swear. I tried to stop him." Todd's eyes shone with tears. Lorelei watched him swallow before he said, "I think he would have wanted me to tell you."

"Thank you, Todd. I'm glad you did," James said.

Lorelei touched the boy's shoulder. "You did the right thing."

He nodded, swallowed a few times and ate the last bite of his sandwich.

She looked across the table at James. He held her gaze until she felt a shudder at what they'd just heard and had to look away.

Chapter Fifteen

"Are you okay?" James asked Lori after Todd left. He'd helped her clear the table, then followed her back into the kitchen.

"Fine," she said, her back to him.

"I forgot about your dinner with your stepmother tonight. I'm sorry. I hope I'm not making you late."

She turned in his direction, avoiding eye contact. "She cancelled. Something came up." He said nothing. Finally, she looked at him. "She's scaring me."

He nodded. "But maybe it has nothing to do with Billy Sherman. At least now we know why Billy went out that night. We just don't know who he was following or why." He sighed. "I'm sorry. I feel like I never should have started this." She didn't exactly disagree with her silence.

"Hey," he said. "How do you feel about a big juicy rib eye out at the steak house? I'm buying."

She smiled and he could tell that she was about to decline when his cell rang. He held up a finger, drew out his phone and, seeing who was calling, said, "I need to take this. Hello?"

"Mr. Colt?"

He smiled to himself. No one called him Mr. Colt. "Yes?"

"My name is Connie Sue Matthews. I heard you have taken over your father's private investigations firm and that you've been asking questions about Billy Sherman's death."

"That's right."

"You probably know I was the one who found the body that morning. Could I stop by your office? I know it's after hours, but it's the only time I'm free this week. I might have some information for you." She lowered her voice. "I don't want to get into it on the phone."

He shot a look at Lori. He'd been looking forward to that steak but had really been looking forward to dinner with her. He hesitated only a moment, hoping Lori would understand. If this woman had any information for him... "You know where my office is?"

"Yes, I can be there in a few minutes."

"Use the back entrance. I'll see you then." He disconnected and looked across the room at Lori. Only moments before he was mentally kicking himself for digging into his father's unsolved case and here he was cancelling his dinner plans because of it. What was wrong with him? "I'm afraid I'm going to have to postpone that dinner invitation."

"Bad news?" she asked, looking genuinely concerned.

"No, maybe just the opposite." He could only hope.

CORA SAT IN the house, the shotgun lying across her lap. All the lights were out and there was no sound except when the refrigerator turned on in the kitchen occasionally. She'd always been a patient woman. She'd put up with her no-account husband for almost fifty years. She could sit here all night if she had to.

But she knew she wouldn't have to. She knew Otis Osterman. He was a hothead without a lot upstairs. He'd stop by tonight and she would be waiting.

The fool would be mad, filled with indignation that she'd called him out. He wouldn't be thinking clearly. She reminded herself to make sure he died in the house after he broke in. She didn't want any trouble with the law—especially Otis's baby brother, Carl. But an old woman like herself had every right to defend her life—and her property.

Otis should have taken her deal. He'd regret it. If he lived that long.

And to think back in grade school she'd had a crush on him. He'd been cute back then, blond with freckles and two missing front teeth. She shook her head at the memory. That was before high school when she found out firsthand about his mean streak. But she'd taken care of it—just as she'd taken care of everything else all these years. If he came around tonight, this time he would leave with more than a scar to remember her by. Or not leave alive at all.

CONNIE MATTHEWS WAS a small immaculate-looking woman in her late fifties. She was clearly nervous as she stepped into his office. He'd had just enough time to pick up the room and close the door to the bedroom before she'd arrived.

She sat on the edge of one of the leather club chairs, her purse gripped in her lap as he sat behind his father's desk. Idly he wondered how long it would take for him to think of this office as his own.

"You said you might have information on Billy Sherman's death?"

Connie looked even more uncomfortable. "Those boys, Billy and that Crane boy. I found them hiding in my bushes one day. They were always sneaking around, getting into trouble, stomping down my poor flowers. One day I caught them going through my garbage! Can you imagine? Billy said they were looking for clues. *Clues.* Clues to what, I'd demanded. And the Crane boy said, 'We know what you've been doing.' Then they laughed and ran off."

It sounded like typical boy stuff to James. He hated to think of some of the shenanigans he and his brothers had pulled. "Did you tell my father about this when he interviewed you?" James knew it wasn't in his father's notes.

She shook her head. "It seemed silly at the time because that young boy had lost his life. But what was he doing out in that storm in the middle of the night in his pajamas?"

"Since your house is the closest to where he was found, did you notice anyone outside that night? Hear anything?" He already knew the answer. *That* was in his father's notes. But Todd said that his friend was following someone.

"No, but I went to bed early. I don't like storms. I took some sleeping pills and didn't wake up until the next morning. By then the storm was over."

"What about your husband?"

"What about him?" Connie asked frowning.

"I wondered if he might have mentioned seeing anyone, hearing anything."

She shook her head. "George went to bed when I did so I'm sure he would have mentioned it, if he had seen someone or heard anything, don't you think? That's a busy road. Gotten even busier with all the houses that have come up. The mayor lives in the new section and I suppose you know that Senator Bayard lives just down the road from our place." She seemed to puff up a little.

That road was an old one used by a lot of residents who lived out that way. The subdivision had grown in the past nine years.

"Was there something more?" he asked. On the phone she'd sounded as if she might have new information. That didn't seem to be the case and yet she was still sitting across from him, still looking nervous and anxious. He waited, something he'd seen his father do during an interview.

"I hate to even bring this up, but I feel I was remiss by not doing it nine years ago," Connie finally said. "I think someone abducted that boy from his bed. Because what boy in his right mind would go out in a storm like that?" she demanded, clearly warming to the subject. "And I know who did it. It was the father." At his confused look, she said, "The *boy's* father, that ne'r-do-well, Sean Sherman. Weren't he and his wife arguing over the boy in the divorce? I think Sean snatched him out of his bed that night. That's why the mother didn't hear anything. The boy would have gone willingly with his own father otherwise he would have raised a ruckus, don't you think?"

"That is one theory. I wonder though how Billy ended up getting run over just blocks from his house?"

"Maybe the boy changed his mind, decided he didn't want to go with him and jumped out of the car. It would be just like his drugged-up father to run over the boy and then panic and take off."

James pretended to take notes, which seemed to please the woman. "I'll look into that," he told her, and she rose to leave, looking relieved.

"I wasn't sure if I should say anything or not," Connie said. "But you haven't been around much so you don't know a lot about this town and the people who live in it. I thought you should know." She let out a breath, nodded and headed for the door where she stopped to look back at him. "I'd be careful if I were you though. If Sean Sherman killed that boy, he thinks he's gotten away with it for nine years." She nodded again as if that said it all, but seemed compelled to add, "I hired Sean one time to do some landscaping. He made a mess of it. When I refused to pay him..." She shuddered. "The man has a terrible temper. He's dangerous."

"Thank you, Mrs. Matthews."

"I believe in doing my civic duty," she said primly and left.

CORA HEARD THE sound of shattering glass in the basement of her small house and smiled. Otis was just too predictable. What was he thinking he was going to do anyway? Kill her? The thought made her laugh. He was a nasty little bugger, but she couldn't see him committing murder. No, he'd come out here to scare her.

She shifted the shotgun in her lap and waited. Her chair was in a corner where she would see him when he came upstairs. She could hear him moving around down there. After tonight, Otis was going to replace that window he'd broken and anything else she wanted done around here.

Over the years, she'd collected a few people who were indebted to her after she'd caught them in some nefarious act. Some paid her monthly, others paid in favors. She didn't like to think of it as blackmail. She preferred to call it penitence for misdeeds done. She never asked for more than a person could afford.

But she didn't like Otis. She would make him pay dearly—if she didn't shoot him on sight.

Her cell phone rang, startling her. She glanced at the time. Almost one in the morning. The phone rang again—and she realized no sound was now coming from the basement.

"Hello?" she whispered into the phone, planning to give whoever was calling a piece of her mind for interrupting her at this hour.

"I got your money," Otis said. "I'll put it in your account tomorrow. Why are you whispering?" He chuckled. "Oh, I hope I didn't wake you up."

She could hear what sounded like bar noise in the background. "Where are you?" she demanded.

"At Harry's as if that is any of your damned business," he snapped and disconnected.

She stared at the phone for a moment. Then she heard

again a sound coming from the basement. Her blood ran cold. If Otis wasn't down there, then who was? Cora felt fear coil around her as she heard a sound she recognized.

A moment later, she smelled the smoke.

Chapter Sixteen

James was awakened some time in the night by the sound of sirens. Sheriff's department patrol SUVs and several fire trucks sped down Main Street and kept going until the sirens died away. He'd rolled over and gone back to sleep until his cell phone rang just after 7:00 a.m.

"Did you hear about the fire?" his friend Ryan asked. "That old busybody crossed the wrong person this time. Cora says someone set her house on fire, but I heard the sheriff's trying to pin it on her. Arson."

"You've heard all this already this morning?"

"The men's coffee clutch down at the cafe. You should join us. It's a lot of the old gang along with some of the old men in town. Pretty interesting stuff most mornings."

James shook his head and told himself he wouldn't be staying in town that long. His leg was better, and his ribs didn't hurt with every breath. It was progress. "Thanks for the invite," he said. "I'll keep it in mind."

"How is the investigation going?"

He was saved from answering as he got another call.

"Sorry, I'm getting another call. Talk to you later?" He didn't wait for an answer as he accepted the call. At first all he heard was coughing, an awful hack that he didn't recognize. "Hello?" he repeated.

"I want to hire you." The words came out strained between coughs. "Someone tried to burn me alive in my own house last night."

"Cora?" The last time she'd said more than a few words to him, she'd been chasing him and his brothers away from her apple trees with a shotgun.

In between coughs, she said, "You're a private detective, aren't you?"

"Isn't the sheriff investigating?" he asked, sitting up to rub a hand over his face. It was too early in the morning for this.

"Carl? That old reprobate!" He waited through a coughing fit. "He thinks I set the fire, that's how good an investigator he is. I put myself in the hospital and burned down my own house? Idiot." More coughing. "You owe me, James Colt, for all the times you and your brothers trespassed in my yard and stole my apples."

He wanted to point out that she'd had more apples than she could ever use and let them waste every year. But they *were* her apples.

"The least you can do is prove that I didn't start the fire. Otherwise, the sheriff is talking putting me behind bars."

"I'll look into it," he said, all the time mentally kicking himself.

"Good. Don't overcharge me."

James disconnected. He lay down again, but he knew

there was no chance he could get back to sleep. After Connie Matthews had left last night, he'd hoped Lori was still around. She wasn't so he'd gone out and gotten himself some fast food and then driven to Billy Sherman's neighborhood.

From there, he'd walked toward the spot where the boy had died. He'd tried to imagine doing the same thing in a violent thunderstorm at the age of seven. Whoever Billy had seen couldn't have been some random person like anyone he and Todd normally followed. The boy must have recognized the person. But then why hadn't he mentioned a name to Todd? Or maybe there was something about the person that had lured him out into the storm. James couldn't imagine what it could have been.

An image from a movie during his own childhood popped into his head of a clown holding a string with a bright-colored balloon floating overhead. It had given him nightmares for weeks. A kid afraid of the dark and storms wouldn't go after a clown—especially one with a balloon.

LORELEI HAD DRIVEN past her stepmother's house last night only to see all the lights were out and her car wasn't in the garage. She'd been tempted to drive out to the senator's house to see if she was there. Earlier this evening on the news she'd heard that the senator and his wife were officially divorcing.

"They reported that they've been separated for some time now and believe it is best if they end the marriage,"

the newscaster had said. *"Senator Bayard said the divorce is amicable and that he wishes only the best for Mary."*

It had sounded as if Mary was the one who'd wanted the separation and divorce. Maybe she had. Maybe Lorelei had been too hard on her stepmother.

The news had ended with a mention of Bayard being called back to Washington on some subcommittee work he was doing. She wondered how true that was. Maybe Fred and her stepmother had flown off somewhere together to celebrate the divorce.

What bothered Lorelei was that her stepmother felt the need to lie to her. Or at the very least not to be honest with her. Like providing the loan for the sandwich shop. Like falling in love without telling her. While Lorelei didn't approve of her stepmother's affair, she wanted her to be happy. She hated the strain in their relationship and promised herself that she would do what she could to fix it when she saw Karen again.

After a restless night, she'd gotten up and gone to work as usual. As she pulled in behind the shop to park, James was standing by the back door of his office grinning.

"My license came today. It's official—I'm a private investigator."

"Congratulations. You'll have to frame it and put it up on your wall."

"I know it seems silly being excited about it, but I am. It makes me feel legit. I also have a new client." She raised a brow. "I'll tell you all about it over dinner. I thought we'd go out and celebrate. I owe you a steak." She started to argue, but he stopped her with a warm hand on her bare arm. "Please? You wouldn't make me celebrate alone, would you?"

She knew he could make a call to any number of women who would jump at a steak dinner date with him. When she'd awakened this morning, she'd promised herself that she would see her stepmother tonight—if her stepmother was in town.

James waved the license in the air and grinned. "How can a Montana girl like you say no to a slab of grain-fed beef grilled over a hot fire?"

Lorelei laughed in spite of her sometime resolve to keep James Colt at arm's length. "Fine. What time?"

JAMES COULDN'T HELP smiling as he drove out to Cora's. Lori had agreed to have dinner with him. He hadn't been this excited about a date in… Heck, he wasn't sure he ever had been. That should have worried him, he realized.

Cora's house had sat on a hill. Smoke was still rising up through the pine trees and into the blue summer sky as he pulled in.

After parking, he got out of his truck and walked over to the firefighters still putting out the last of the embers. One of the fears of living in the pine trees was always fire. But the firefighters had been able to contain the blaze from spreading into the pines. The small old house though seemed to be a total loss.

"I'm looking for the arson investigator," James said and was pointed to a man wearing a mask and gloves and a Montana State University Bobcats baseball cap digging around in the ashes.

"I'm Private Detective James Colt," he said introducing himself.

The man gave him a glance and continued digging. "Colt? That your property next door?"

"Yep."

"A lot of recent fires out here." He rose to his feet and extended a gloved hand before drawing it back to wipe soot onto his pants. "Sorry about that. Gil Sanders."

James couldn't help his surprise. "Gilbert Sanders?" he asked, remembering seeing the name on his father's list. But why would his father be interested in talking to an arson investigator as part of Billy Sherman's hit-and-run?

"Have we met before?" Gil asked, studying him. "You look familiar."

"My father, PI Del Colt, might have contacted you about another investigation."

The man frowned. "Sorry. Can you be more specific?"

"He was investigating the hit-and-run death of a local boy about nine years ago."

Gil shook his head. "You're sure it was me he spoke with?"

"Maybe not." Now that James thought about it, there hadn't been any notes from the interview in his father's file. "I'm here about another matter. Cora Brooks called me this morning. Anything new on the fire?"

"It was definitely arson. The blaze was started in the basement. The accelerant was gasoline. It burned hot and fast. She was lucky to get out alive."

James nodded. "The sheriff seemed to think Cora started the fire herself."

The investigator shook his head. "I've already reviewed the statements from the first responders. The property owner was in a robe and slippers carrying a shotgun and a pair of binoculars. That's all she apparently managed to save. She couldn't have outrun that fire if she started it. Not in those slippers. I'm told she is in her right mind."

"Sharp and lethal as a new filet knife."

Gil chuckled. "She told first responders that she'd heard someone breaking into her basement. That's why she had her shotgun. Not sure why the binoculars were so important to her, but I don't see any way a woman her age could have started the fire in the basement and hightailed it upstairs to an outside deck. Not with as much gas as was used downstairs. I'm not even sure she can lift the size gas can that was found."

Cora was apparently in the clear. "Thank you. If I figure out why I saw your name in my father's case file…"

"Just give me a call. But unless it pertains to a fire, I can't imagine why he had wanted to talk to me."

James shook the man's hand and nodded at Gil's cap. "Go Bobcats," he said and headed back to his pickup. Too bad all his PI cases weren't this easy, he thought. He headed for the hospital to give Cora the good news. This one was on him, no charge. He knew she'd like the sound of that.

OTIS STUMBLED TO his cabin door hungover, half-asleep and ticked off. Whoever was pounding on his door was going to regret it.

"What the hell did you do?" his brother Carl demanded, pushing past him and into the cabin. The sheriff turned to look at him and swore. "On second thought, I don't want to know."

"If this is about that fire out at Cora's—"

"What else? I saw you yesterday. You were going on about the woman and last night her house burns down." Carl raised a hand. "There's an arson investigator out there. I told him that I think Cora did it for the insurance money, but he sure as the devil isn't going to take my word for it."

"I didn't do it." Otis stepped past him to open the refrigerator. He needed the hair of the dog that bit him last night. Pulling out a can of beer he popped the top, took a long drink and looked at his brother.

"How deep are you in all this?" Carl demanded.

"I did something stupid."

His brother groaned. "I wouldn't be here if I didn't suspect that was the case."

"I took something out to the Colt place. I was going to make an anonymous call and let you find it. I know you'd like to get that arrogant little turd behind bars as much as I would."

The sheriff swore. "Tell me it isn't anything explosive. You get anyone killed—"

"No, just some illegal stuff. Doesn't matter now. I'll get it hauled away. It was stupid. Then Cora saw me, said she made a video of me dumping it…" He hung his head again.

"Otis, swear to me you didn't burn down Cora's house."

The former sheriff looked up, his expression one of disbelief and hurt. "I was at the bar. You can check. I was there until closing. Even better about the time it was catching fire, I called Cora from the bar. See I have an alibi so I'm gold."

His brother swore.

"What's wrong? There will be a record of the call—just before I heard the sirens. So it couldn't have been me."

Carl told himself that his brother had been at the bar to establish that alibi, which meant Otis had hired someone to set fire to the place. He wished he didn't know his brother so well. "If it wasn't you, any idea who might have wanted Cora dead?"

Otis chuckled. "Anyone who's ever crossed her path."

"Let's just hope Gil Sanders doesn't find any evidence out there that would make him think you had anything to do with this."

CORA TOOK THE news as would be expected. She nodded, told James he'd better not send her a bill and ordered him out of her room.

A near-death experience didn't change everyone apparently, he thought as he left chuckling.

He was still wondering if the Gilbert Sanders on his father's list was the arson investigator and if so what Del thought the man could offer on the hit-and-run case.

Meanwhile, he tracked down Sean Sherman. His call went straight to voice mail. He left a message asking Sean to call him and hung up. Sherman lived in a town not far from Lonesome. If he had to, James would drive over and pay the man a visit.

With that done, he considered his father's list again. Connie Matthews had said something in her original interview with his father that kept bothering him. Lyle Harris had been operating the front-end loader the morning Connie had seen the body and stopped him from covering it up.

James knew it was a long shot. His father had already talked to the man and there wasn't anything in his notes that sent up a red flag. But he was running out of people to interview and getting worried that he'd missed something important.

At forty-five, Lyle Harris had quit his job with the local contractor after a work comp accident that had put him in a wheelchair. As James pulled up out front of his place deep in the woods, he noticed the ramp from the house through the carport to the garage. He recalled Ryan telling him that he'd donated the lumber and the men Lyle used to work with had donated their time to make the house more wheelchair accessible.

After parking, he got out and walked toward the house, changing directions as he heard the whine of an electric saw coming from the garage.

"Lyle!" he called. "Lyle, it's James Colt!" The sound of the saw stopped abruptly. He heard what sounded like a cry of pain and quickly stepped through the door into the large garage.

The first thing he saw was the wheelchair lying on its side. Past it, he caught movement as someone ran out the back door and into the pines. He charged into the garage thinking it had been Lyle who'd run out.

But he hadn't gone far when he saw that Lyle had left a bloody trail on the concrete floor where he'd crawled away from the wheelchair, away from the electric saw lying on the floor next to it, the blade dripping blood.

"What the hell?" he said, rushing to the man on the floor. He was already digging out his phone to call 911.

"No, don't. Please. Don't call. I'm okay," Lyle cried as he pressed a rag against the wound that had torn through his jeans to the flesh of his lower leg. "It's not fatal."

James stared at the man, then slowly disconnected before the 911 operator answered. "I just saw someone running out of here. What's going on?"

Lyle shook his head. "Could you get my chair?"

He walked over, picked it up and rolled the wheelchair over to the man, holding it steady as Lyle lifted himself into it.

"It looks worse than it is," Lyle said as he rolled over to a low workbench. He grabbed a first aid kit. "But thanks for showing up when you did."

"That blade could have taken off your leg," James said.

"Naw, it wouldn't have gone that far."

Lyle winced as he poured rubbing alcohol on the wound then began to bandage it with shaking fingers. From what James could tell, the man was right. The wound wasn't deep. "You want help with that?"

"No. I'm fine," he said, turning his back to him.

"You're in trouble." Lyle said nothing. "And whatever it is, it's serious." James took a guess on how many times he'd seen Lyle's rig parked in front of the casino since he'd been back in town. "Gambling?"

Lyle finished and spun the wheelchair around to face him. "I appreciate you stopping by when you did. Now what can I do for you?"

He sighed. His father used to say that you couldn't help people who didn't want to be helped. He knew that to be true. He chewed at his cheek for a moment, thinking. "Were you gambling nine years ago when Billy Sherman died?"

The question took the man by surprise.

James saw the answer in Lyle's face and swore. "Connie Matthews said that if she hadn't seen Billy Sherman's body lying in that ditch when she did, you would have dumped dirt on him with your front-end loader and he would never have been found. She also told my father that she'd been surprised that you were already working that morning since you usually didn't start that early. In fact, she'd been afraid you were going to get fired since she'd heard Edgar Appleton, your boss, warning you before that day about coming to work late so often. She thought that's why you were there so early that morning and that still half-asleep, you didn't see the boy and would have buried him in that ditch. You would have known that the concrete had been ordered for the driveway. It was going to be delivered that day. Had you covered Billy's body with dirt, it would have never have been found."

Lyle stared him down for a full minute. "Like I said, thanks for stopping by."

"I don't believe you ran that boy down, but I do wonder if you weren't hired to get rid of his body. Maybe hired is the wrong word. Coerced into making Billy Sherman disappear?"

"You can see your way out," Lyle said, wheeling around and heading toward his house.

Chapter Seventeen

Lorelei couldn't believe that she'd agreed to have dinner with James. He'd caught her at a weak moment. The small table at the back of the steak house was dimly lit. A single candle flickered from a ceramic cowboy boot at the center. The candlelight made his blue eyes sparkle more than usual and brought out the shine of his thick dark hair.

If she had been on a real date, it would have been romantic. But this was James. A woman would be a fool to take him seriously.

James lifted his wineglass in a toast, those blue eyes taking her captive. "Thank you for indulging me tonight."

"My pleasure," she said automatically and realized she meant it as she lifted her own wineglass and tapped it gently against his. She couldn't remember the last dinner date she'd been on with a man. She took a sip of the wine. It was really good. "I'm surprised you know your wines."

He grinned. "You're impressed, aren't you?" He

shook his head. "I called earlier and talked to the sommelier. I didn't want to look like a dumb cowboy."

"You could never be a dumb cowboy," she said, feeling the alcohol loosen her tongue. She'd have to be careful tonight. The candlelight, the soft music, the wine, the company, it made her want to let her hair down—so to speak. She'd pulled her hair up as per usual, but in a softer twist. She'd worn a favorite dress that she'd been told looked good on her and she'd spritzed on a little perfume behind each ear.

She felt James's intent gaze on her a moment before he said, "You look beautiful." His tone sent a tremor through her that jump-started her heart.

Lorelei sipped her wine, fighting for a control she didn't feel. "Thank you. I could say the same about you." He'd worn all black from his button-up shirt to his jeans to his new boots. The outfit accented his long muscular legs and cupped a behind that could have sold a million pairs of jeans. The black Western shirt was opened just enough to expose the warm glow of his throat and make her yearn to see more.

There'd been a time when she'd dreamed of being with James Colt. When she'd fantasized what it would be like if he ever asked her out. But he never had. Until now. She had to remind herself that this wasn't a real date and yet it certainly felt real the way he was looking at her.

She was surprised to see that she'd finished her wine. James started to refill her glass—and not for the first time. She shook her head. Given the trail her thoughts had taken, the last thing she needed was more wine.

James suddenly got to his feet and reached for her hand. "Dance with me."

She took his hand before the words registered. Dance? She glanced at the intimate dance floor as he drew her to her feet. No one was dancing. But he was already leading her to it. He turned her to the middle of the dance floor and pulled her directly into his arms.

He drew her close and she let him. She pressed her cheek against his shoulder knowing she couldn't blame the wine. Their bodies moved in time to the music as if they were one of those older couples who'd danced together for decades.

Lorelei drew back a little to look into his eyes and wanted to pinch herself. Not even in her fantasies had she dreamed of James Colt holding her in his arms and looking at her like this. She'd been only a girl and, like her Barbie dolls, she'd long ago stored all that away. And yet here they were.

She pressed her cheek against his warm shoulder again, closed her eyes and let herself enjoy this moment. Because that's all it was. A moment. Just like in the closet with him. The memory made her smile. He'd actually been embarrassed by his reaction to her.

The song ended. There was that awkward moment when they stood looking into each other's eyes. She was certain that he wanted to kiss her, but the waiter came by with their salads. The moment gone.

Her heart was still triple-timing as James walked her back to the table, holding her hand, squeezing it before letting it go.

"You dance well," she said.

He grinned. "My brother Willie taught me."

She laughed and felt herself relax a little. He had been about to kiss her, hadn't he? Another awkward moment before they dug into their salads, both seemingly lost in their private thoughts.

By the time their meals came they were talking like friends who owned businesses next door to each other. They'd both grown up in Lonesome so it made it easy to talk about the past and stay away from the future. That moment on the dance floor had passed as if it had never happened. She suspected they both were glad of that. Otherwise, it could have made being business neighbors awkward. Neither of them wanted that.

ASKING LORI TO dance had been a mistake. Not that James hadn't enjoyed having her in his arms. He'd loved the sweet scent of her, nuzzling his way into her hair to get at its source behind her ears. She'd smelled heavenly. She'd felt heavenly.

He'd lost himself in the feel of her, wishing the song would never end. It was as if they'd called a truce, shared no uncomfortable past, had only this amazing few minutes moving together as one, in perfect sync.

And then the song ended and he'd looked at her and all he'd wanted to do was kiss her. She'd parted those lips as if expecting the kiss. He'd seen something in her eyes, a fire burning like the one burning inside him. And then the waiter had been forced to go around them to put their salads on their table and he was reminded of all the reasons he shouldn't get involved with this woman. He wasn't staying. Getting the PI license was a hoot, but he was a rodeo cowboy. If he solved this case, then it would make all of this worthwhile. But once he was healed, he would be leaving again. Long-distance relationships didn't work. Just ask Melody.

But all that aside, he'd mentally kicked himself for not kissing her when he had the chance. Maybe he'd known deep inside that once he kissed her there was no going back with this one. Lori wasn't like anyone he'd dated—if you could even call it dating. The others had known what they were getting into and had ridden in eyes wide open.

Lori was different. She expected more. Would want more from him. More than he had to give at this point in his life. One of these days he'd think about settling down, but he hoped those days were still a long way off.

Even as he thought it, he couldn't help looking over at Lori as he walked her to her door later that night. He felt the pull of something stronger than the road, maybe even stronger than the rodeo, stronger than even his resolve.

"Thank you for a lovely evening and congratulations again," she said as she pulled out her keys and turned to unlock her door.

He didn't feel like himself as he touched her arm and gently turned her back toward him. "Lori." It didn't feel like his arms that drew her to him. Or his lips that dropped hungrily to her mouth. Or his fingers that released her hair and let it fall in waves of chestnut down her slim back.

Her perfume filled his senses as her arms looped around his neck and he pushed his body into hers until the only way they could have been closer was naked in the throws of passionate lovemaking.

The kiss and that thought sent a bolt of desire rocketing through him. He had never wanted a woman like he did this one. He felt humbled with desire. He wanted to be a better man. He wanted to be her man. He wanted her. For keeps.

He felt her palms on his chest, felt her gentle push as she drew her mouth from his and leaned back to look into his eyes. He saw naked desire as well as the battle going on there. She was as scared as he was.

She shook her head slowly. Regretfully? And pulled free of his arms. He watched her straighten, brushing her long hair back as she lifted the keys in her hand and turned toward the door again.

He let her fumble with the key to the lock for a moment before he took the keys from her and opened her door. Then desire still raging through him, he handed her the keys and took a step back. He feared that if he took her in his arms again there really would be no turning back. He looked at her and knew he couldn't do it. He wouldn't let himself hurt this woman.

"Thanks again for tonight," he said, his voice rough with emotion. "I'll see you tomorrow." He turned and hurried down the steps to his pickup. He hadn't noticed the car that had gone by. Hadn't heard it. Only the taillights turning in the distance made him even aware that anyone had driven past. Nor did he give it more than a distracted notice as he climbed behind the wheel and, thinking of Lori, allowed himself to glance back at the house.

She was no longer standing there, thank goodness. The door was closed and a light glowed deep in the house. He sat for a moment, still shaken before he started the engine and headed toward home, knowing he wouldn't be able to sleep a wink.

But to his surprise, he fell asleep the moment his head hit the pillow only to be assaulted by dreams that wove themselves together in a jumbled pattern that felt too real and too frightening. In the dream, he'd known that it wasn't just him who was in danger. Lori was there and he was having trouble getting to her when the little blond-haired girl appeared on her horse. She was laughing and smiling as she cantered toward him. "Watch this, Daddy!"

He half woke in a sweat. The nightmare clung to him, holding him under even as he tried to surface. He was in uncharted waters on a leaky boat and it was impossible to swim with the concrete blocks that were tied to his ankles.

Chapter Eighteen

Lorelei woke and panicked for a moment, thinking she was late for work. She hadn't gotten to sleep until very late last night. It had taken her a while to process everything. James had kissed her. He'd called her Lori in a way that made her heart race. No one had ever given her a nickname. She hadn't been that kind of girl. Until James.

And that was the problem. He'd upset her orderly world. He'd made her burn inside with a need she knew only he could fulfill. He'd made her want to throw caution to the wind.

And then he'd been a perfect gentleman, unlocking her front door, handing her the keys and leaving.

She'd been shocked. But mostly…disappointed. She hadn't planned to invite him in. But he hadn't even tried. A man with his reputation? Surely, he had to know the power he had over women. He would know she was vulnerable after a kiss like that. So why hadn't he asked to spend the night?

Lorelei knew it was ridiculous that she was angry with him for not hitting on her. Everything the man seemed to do made her angry with him, even when he was well-behaved. Maybe it wasn't him. Maybe it was her who was the problem. Maybe he didn't find her attractive.

Those thoughts had her tossing and turning and losing sleep because of him. That too annoyed her with him.

She told herself that her life had been just fine before he'd showed up next door. Her stepmother was right. Having James Colt living next to her shop was a bad idea. The man was too...distracting.

As daylight crept into the room, she lay in bed staring up at the ceiling reliving the kiss, reliving the way he'd cupped the back of her neck, the way he'd buried his face in her hair, the way he said Lori.

"Oh, for crying out loud!" she snapped and swung her legs over the side of the bed. She was acting like a teenager.

The thought actually made her smile. She'd been so driven from middle school on that all she'd thought about was excelling in her school work so she could get into a good college. Then at college she'd worked hard to get top grades so she could get a good job. She hadn't let herself be a teenager and do what a lot of other teenagers did—like James Colt.

She'd missed so much. No wonder she'd never felt like this, she realized. Until now. Now she wanted it all. And she wanted it with James.

He had wanted her, hadn't he? That kiss... She'd seen the desire in his blue eyes. So why had he just walked away last night?

Because for the first time maybe in his entire life he was being sensible, something she'd been her whole life? Oh, that was so like him, she thought angrily as she stepped into the shower. *Now* he decided to be responsible.

JAMES THREW HIMSELF into work the next morning. His thoughts and emotions had been all over the place from the moment he'd opened his eyes. The cold shower he'd taken hadn't helped so he'd left the office early to avoid seeing Lori.

He knew it was cowardice, but after that kiss last night he didn't trust himself around her. That had been a first for him. Normally after a kiss like that, he would only avoid a woman if he didn't want to see her again. But Lori wasn't just some woman and that was the problem.

Because it was Montana, the drive to the next town gave him plenty of time to think—more than an hour and a half. In this part of the state, the towns were few and far between.

Alice Sherman's ex worked as a maintenance man at the local hospital. As it turned out, today was Sean's day off. A helpful employee told him that the man lived only a block away in a large apartment house.

James walked, needing to clear his head. On the drive over, he'd had plenty of time to think. Too much. He'd finally turned on a country station on the radio. Not that even music could get his mind off Lori Wilkins.

He went from wishing he hadn't come back to town to being grateful that he had because of her. He went from wishing he could get right back on the rodeo circuit to being too involved in not just this case to want to leave now. He knew the best thing he could do was give Lori a wide berth, but at the same time, he couldn't wait to see her again.

Now as he shoved open the front door of the large apartment house, he tried to focus on work. According to the mailboxes by the door, Sherman was in 322. He turned toward the large old elevator and decided to take the stairs.

The man who answered the door at 322 was tall and slim and nice-looking. He was nothing like James had been expecting. Nor was the man's apartment. It was neat and clean, much like the man himself. "May I help you?"

"I'm James Colt. I'm a private investigator in Lonesome."

"Did Alice hire you?"

"No. I believe my father, Del Colt, was hired by you to look into the death of your son. As you know, he died before he finished the case. I've taken it over. I'd like to ask you a few questions."

Sean Sherman seemed to be making up his mind. After a moment, he stepped back. "Come on in. I'm not sure how I can help," he said after they were seated in the living room. "Alice and I were separated at the time and in the middle of a divorce. I was fighting for joint custody, but I would imagine she already told you that." She hadn't, but James had read as much in his father's notes.

"Were you in Lonesome that night?"

The man hesitated a little too long so James was surprised when he finally answered. "Yes." That definitely wasn't what Sean had told Del.

"You were?"

Sean sighed before he said, "I lied to your father about that. I had my reasons at the time."

"Then why tell me the truth now?"

"Because if it will help you find out who killed my son, then nothing else matters."

"But that wasn't the case nine years ago?" James asked.

"Other people were involved. It was a very traumatic time in my life. The divorce, arguing over Billy. I don't know if Alice told you this or not." He met James's gaze and held it. "I was having an affair. Alice found out and our marriage was over. The affair was a mistake, one I will always regret. I didn't want all of that made public and having it thrown in Alice's face. We'd lost our son. We were both devastated. The rest of it wasn't important."

"I understand drugs were involved?"

"I'll be honest with you. I couldn't take the pain of what I'd done, blamed myself for not being in the house with my family that night and I turned to drugs. It's taken me a long time to climb back out of that. Being honest is part of my recovery."

"If you were in Lonesome that night, but not at your house, where were you?" James asked.

Sean looked away for a moment before he said, "I was at Karen Wilkins's house."

He couldn't help his surprise. "She was the woman you were having the affair with?"

The man nodded. "I was in the middle of breaking it off with her."

"Were you there all night?" James asked.

"I think so. Things got very emotional. Karen left. She ran out into the storm. I started to go after her but turned back."

"She left on foot?"

He nodded. "But not long after that I heard her take her car and leave."

"What time was that?"

"I think it was about ten."

"You didn't go after her in your car?" Sean shook his head. "When did she come back?"

"I don't know exactly. I got into her booze, got disgustingly drunk and passed out; and when I woke up, she was standing over me distraught, screaming, crying and telling me to get out. It was daylight by then. I left and the only time I went back to Lonesome was for my son's funeral. I tried to mend things with Alice but…" He shook his head. "That's it."

James thought about it for a moment. "When you woke to find Karen home again what kind of shape was she in? I know she was upset. There was a thunderstorm that night. Was she still wet from being out in it?"

The man frowned. "No. Her clothes must have dried because they weren't wet. Stranger was the fact that she'd fixed her hair. She had to have been home for a while, I guess." He shook his head. "You can tell how out of it I was."

"She was wearing the same clothing though?"

"She was. She had to have been home for a while before she woke me up. I could tell that she'd had a shower." He shrugged. "I liked the smell of her shower gel."

James shook his head. If he knew anything about women who felt scorned, it was that they didn't calmly come home shower, fix their hair, put on the same clothing and then decide to wake you up to throw you out. So where had Karen been that she'd spent the night, taken a shower and gotten her clothes dried? He supposed it was possible that she'd gone to her exercise studio. They probably had showers there. Karen could even have a washer and dryer down there for all he knew. Still, it seemed odd.

"Did you hear any more from her?" he asked.

Sean shook his head. "That night pretty well ended everything in Lonesome for me."

"She's never tried to contact you?"

"Never. Nor did I ever contact her. It was over almost before it started. We both regretted it. I'm sure I could have handled it better than I did."

James thanked the man and showed himself out. He couldn't help being surprised about Karen. But at least now he knew why she was on his father's list. She'd been upset and out driving that night in the storm. Had she done something? Had she seen something?

He felt a start. But how had Del found out about her possible involvement in Billy's death? Sean hadn't told him and Karen certainly hadn't shared the information when James had tried to question her.

Had someone seen her that night?

LORELEI DID WHAT she always did on Sunday morning. She went to church; only today she was asked to help with the toddlers in child care during the service and jumped at it. She loved the job, especially toddler age. They were so much fun as they raced around, laughing and screaming and keeping her on her toes. Seriously, she later thought. What had she been thinking volunteering for this since she had thirteen toddlers between her and another volunteer? It was wonderful madness.

For several hours she forgot about everything, especially James.

Then it ended, parents picked up their children and she was facing what she did at home each Sunday after church: cleaning house. Today, the place got an extra good scrubbing even though it didn't need it. Her house was small—just the way she liked it since she spent so little time there.

She'd just finished when her doorbell rang. Her first thought was that it was probably her stepmother. They often did something together on a Sunday every month or so. But when she opened the door, it was James standing there. She blinked in surprise and then horror as she realized what she was wearing. Leggings and an oversized sweatshirt that hung off one shoulder. Her hair was pulled up in a high ponytail. She never wore much makeup, but now she wore none. And she smelled like cleaning solution.

"We need to talk," he said without preamble as he stepped in, seemingly not even noticing her appearance.

"Iced tea or beer?" she asked as she followed him into the kitchen.

"Beer." He looked around. "Nice house."

"Thanks." She took two beers from the refrigerator and handed him one as she led the way into the small living room and curled up on one end of the couch. He took the chair next to it, looking uncomfortable.

"If this is about last night—"

"No," he said too quickly. "I mean." He met her gaze. "No. It's about your stepmother." Lorelei groaned inwardly and thought, *Now what?* "I drove over to Big Timber and talked to Sean Sherman this morning."

She frowned. "Billy's dad?"

He nodded. "He told me something. Are you aware that your stepmother was seeing him nine years ago?"

James could have told her almost anything about her stepmother and she wouldn't have batted an eye. Karen had proven to her how little she knew about the woman who'd raised her.

"What do you mean 'seeing' him?" When James merely looked at her, she let out a cry and shot to her feet. "If you're trying to tell me that my stepmother is a serial philanderer with married men..."

"It might be worse than that," he said. "Sean told me he broke up with her that night. Upset, Karen left the house in the storm, at first on foot, but later came back for her car."

Lorelei had moved to the fireplace but now put her free hand over her mouth, her eyes filling with tears as her heart dropped like a stone, bottoming out.

"We don't know that she was the one who hit Billy—" he choked out. "But she went somewhere. When she returned to her house, she'd either gone straight to the shower, fixed her hair and dried her clothing and put on the same outfit before confronting Sean who'd passed out after being into her booze, or..."

She rolled her eyes. "Or what?"

"She'd been somewhere and showered and fixed her hair before returning to the house to make it look as if she'd been home longer than she had."

Lorelei removed her hand from her mouth and took a drink of her beer without tasting it. She thought she might throw up. "All you have is Sean's word for this, right?" she asked, already looking, hoping, for a way that none of this could be true.

"He's on the wagon, in a program that requires him to be honest, he said, which is why he was willing to talk now. I called Alice on my way back. It's true."

"What am I supposed to say?" she asked, her voice breaking.

"I'm worried about your stepmother. Do you have any idea where she is?" She shook her head. "I've been trying to reach her. From what I can tell she hasn't been home. Neither has the senator."

"Maybe they ran away together to celebrate his divorce," she said. "She thinks he's going to marry her."

"I hope she is with him. I would hate to think that she's alone. It might be my fault that she's left town. I need her side of the story."

Lorelei couldn't believe this and yet she could. It explained why her stepmother had gotten so upset that James was digging into the old hit-and-run case. Because she had a whole lot to hide. But Lorelei couldn't let herself think that her stepmother had killed that boy. She wouldn't.

"I'm sorry to be the one to tell you," he said, sounding as miserable as he looked. "I wish…" He shook his head. He didn't need to say it. She had her wishes too.

She put down her half-full beer. "I'll let you know when I hear from her."

James finished his beer, set the empty bottle on the small table by the chair and rose. He had taken off his Stetson when he'd come in. It now dangled in his fingers by the brim. She couldn't help but think about those fingers on her face, in her hair, last night as he'd kissed her. He'd been so gentle, his caress soft, his callused fingertips sending shivers through her.

He took a step toward her. She couldn't move, couldn't breathe, couldn't think. She felt her eyes widen as he leaned toward her and brushed his lips over hers. "About last night," he said, his voice low. "It was the best date I've ever had." He drew back, his gaze locking with hers before he turned and left.

Chapter Nineteen

James felt as if he'd been kicked in the gut by a bronc. But he'd come this far. He couldn't stop now. He had to finish his father's case. That meant finding Billy Sherman's killer—no matter where the path led him.

When his phone rang, he hoped it would be Lorelei. If not her, then her stepmother. But it was Lyle Harris.

"I've been thinking. I want to talk," Lyle said. "Can you come here?"

"I'm on my way." He turned and went back the way he'd come, turning and going east on a dirt road until he came to the small homemade sign that marked the way into Harris's place hidden in the pines.

James tried not to be anxious, but he'd known that there was more to Lyle's story. He'd just never thought he was going to hear it. Because Lyle was afraid of the person who'd hired him to cover up the body? Or out of loyalty to that person? Either way, James thought, he needed a break in this case. And this just might be it.

He parked, got out and checked the garage shop first before going up to the side door of the house. At his knock, Lyle called, "Come in."

Shoving open the door, he stepped first into a mud room, then a hallway with a lot of doors. "Lyle?" No answer. He felt his skin prickle as he realized belatedly that he might be walking into a trap. The garage had been large, easy to see if someone had been hiding to jump him.

You're getting awfully paranoid.

"In the kitchen," came Lyle's voice.

He headed slowly down the hall, pushing aside half-open doors on his way. True to his word, Lyle was in the kitchen, which had been remodeled to accommodate a man in a wheelchair.

"I was just making chili," Lyle said, his back to him. "My stepmother said no one eats chili in the summer." He turned then to look at James. "I do." Wheeling back to the pot on the stove, he stirred, turned down the heat, and putting down the spoon spun around. He looked nervous, which made James nervous too. "I called you at a weak moment. I'd just talked to my mom on the phone."

"Does that mean that you've changed your mind about telling me the truth?" James said, hoping that's all there was to this.

"Look, I know you're going to keep digging. I've heard around town. A lot of people are getting upset."

"They shouldn't be unless they have something to hide."

Lyle laughed. "Hey, in case you haven't noticed, Lonesome is a small town. It's tight, man. I don't think you realize the position you're in. This is dangerous because you've stirred things up after nine long years when everyone thought it was over."

"Why would they think that? Billy Sherman's killer was never found. Why would people not want the boy's killer to be found?"

"I'm going to level with you," Lyle said. "I think you're an okay dude. Well-meaning enough but treading where you shouldn't be treading unless you have a death wish. So, you're right. I *was* told to cover up the body in the ditch before anyone saw it—especially the neighbors' kids. But I was told it was a coyote."

"A coyote?"

"I saw the blood on the road where it had been hit that morning when I came to work. I had no reason to think otherwise. It was god-awful early in the morning. I was half asleep, half loaded too. I climbed up on my front loader—"

"You didn't go look at the coyote?"

"Why would I? I just loaded up the bucket and was about to dump it when that woman came out and started screaming. That's the truth."

James realized that he believed him. "There's just one thing you left out. Who told you it was a coyote?"

Lyle looked down at his feet for a long moment. "You see all these ramps out here? You see this kitchen? You think the state picked up the bill?" He shook his head. "My friends and the people I worked with did all this."

James felt an icy chill begin to work its way up his spine. "You ever think that the person who told you to bury the...coyote...was lying to you?"

Lyle met his gaze with an angry one. "No, I did not.

Because I admire the hell out of the man who told me to do it. It's the kind of thing he would think to do if he saw a dead coyote in the road in a nice neighborhood where he thought it might upset the kids. You think he would have done that if it had been a little boy lying in that road?"

"I don't know. I guess it depends on who we're talking about." He watched Lyle's temper rise and fall before the man turned back to his chili. James thought he knew where this was headed. He didn't want it to be the man and his wife that he'd had dinner with a few nights ago. He didn't want to believe it and yet he knew that Lyle couldn't be talking about anyone else.

"Edgar told you about the coyote, didn't he? He's the one who told you to come in early and cover it up. You didn't question it because you'd been coming in late and he'd been threatening to fire you. And like you said, you would do anything he asked you—even before your accident."

"It *was* a coyote," Lyle said as if trying to convince himself. "You say otherwise and you're going to destroy a good man. You don't want to do that in this town unless you're planning to leave and never come back. It might already be too late anyway."

James left the man to his chili, hearing the warning, knowing well enough how small towns worked. He suspected his father had made an enemy while working the case and it had gotten him killed.

He felt sick at the thought of Edgar Appleton being involved. He was thinking of the dinner that night, the love he saw between husband and wife, as he climbed into his pickup and started the engine. He didn't want to believe it. Worse, he didn't want to confront the man. Edgar and Irene were good people. But his father always said that even good people made bad decisions and ended up doing bad things sometimes.

Still… He'd turned around and driven through the dense pines toward the main road when he heard it. A rustling sound followed by the distinct rattle. His blood froze as his gaze shot to the passenger side floorboards of his pickup.

He hadn't noticed the paper sack when he'd gotten in. His mind had been on what Lyle had told him. Now though, it drew his attention like a laser as the head of the rattlesnake slithered out, its body coiling, the head rising as the rattles reached a deafening sound.

James slammed on the brakes, throwing the pickup into Park as he flung open the door and bailed out. Even as he did he felt the snake strike his lower calf, sinking its fangs into the top of his cowboy boot.

Chapter Twenty

As Edgar Appleton opened the door, James grabbed his hand and dropped eleven rattles into his palm. He saw the man's startled expression. "What the—"

"Someone put a rattlesnake in my pickup," James said and reached down to draw up his jeans pant leg to show where the snake had almost bitten through the top of his boot before he'd dragged it out and killed it, cutting off the rattles. "Want to guess why?"

The older man frowned. "If you're suggesting—"

"I was at Lyle Harris's house when the snake was put in my pickup. Nine years ago, you told Lyle Harris to bury the body."

Edgar blinked. "You should come in. Irene is out working in the garden. I can see that we need to talk." He turned and walked into the dining room.

Through the window, James could see Irene bent over weeding in the huge garden. He turned to Edgar, wishing this hadn't brought him to this house of all places. He waited, sick at heart.

The older man sighed and dropped into a chair, motioning for James to take one as well. But he was too anxious to sit. He stood near the window and kept waiting.

"Irene and I had been to a movie and stopped for milkshakes at the In-N-Out. We were headed back. It was pouring rain. Irene was driving. There was a car pulled off to the side of the road. Irene went around it and hadn't gone far when she hit something. She stopped, terrified of what she might have run over. We'd both been distracted by the car beside the road. Because of the storm, I had wanted to stop and see if the person needed help, but Irene was anxious to get home. She was worried that she'd left the oven on." He rubbed a hand over his face.

"You didn't check to see what she'd hit?"

"Of course I did," Edgar snapped. "I got out and ran back through the rain. I knew it hadn't been a person. It had been too small." He looked up at James, holding his gaze with a steady one of his own. "It was a coyote. I shoved it off the road. On the way home, I got to thinking about all those kids in that neighborhood seeing it on their way to school. Coyotes remind me of the dogs I've had over my life. So I called Lyle and told him to come in early and make sure it was buried before anyone got up."

"How did the coyote turn into a little boy's broken body?"

"I don't know." He lowered his voice, looked toward the garden. Irene still had her back to them. "I'm telling you the truth."

James didn't know what to believe. "What time was this?"

"A little after ten, I think."

"Did you see anyone else out that night? Did you see Billy?"

"No one other than the car pulled off the road."

"You didn't notice who was in the car or the make or model?"

"It was an SUV, like half the town drives. On top of that the night was pitch-black and with it raining hard... It was tough enough to see anything that night." Edgar swore. "Don't look at me like that. I can tell the difference between a coyote and a kid." His voice broke. "When I heard the news about Billy Sherman..." He looked out the window to the garden. "Irene was beside herself. My wife didn't even believe me. She really thought that I would cover up that child's death to protect her."

"I think you would too," James said. "But if you had, I think it would have eaten you up inside after all these years. I also don't think Irene would have let you."

The older man nodded, smiling sadly. "You're right about that. I'd hoped your father would find out who did it." He met James's gaze. "Find out who killed that boy. Do it for all our sakes."

He saw Irene headed back in. "About the snake—"

"I'll talk to my guys, if that helps, but Lyle has some of his own friends who I have no control over."

"Thanks. Give Irene my regards," he said and left.

LORELEI HAD ALREADY made up her mind that if she didn't hear from her stepmother today she was going to track her down. The day seemed to drag even though she was busy most of it. She was still reeling from what she'd learned from James about Karen and Sean Sherman. How could you think you knew someone so well, only to realize it was a lie?

All day long she'd thought James might stop in for a sandwich. He didn't. She wondered if he was avoiding her. Or just busy with his case. He'd already dug up so much about her stepmother, she feared it would get worse. So maybe not seeing him was good news.

That evening as she locked up, she noted that James's pickup wasn't parked out back. She felt a strange tremor of worry that something might have happened to him. Since he started asking questions about Billy Sherman's death, at least one person had been murdered.

She was almost to her stepmother's house when she saw her pull in. The garage door went up and her stepmother's car disappeared inside. Lorelei pulled in as the garage door closed. She didn't know what she was going to say now that she was here. Accuse Karen of yet another affair? Or of murder and covering it up?

Maybe all her stepmother had been hiding was her relationship with Billy Sherman's father and the divorce that followed. But was there more? Lorelei feared there was.

She climbed out of her SUV and walked to the front door. She didn't have to knock. The door opened and her stepmother was standing there with such a resigned look on her face that Lorelei wanted to cry.

Without a word, Karen stepped back to let her in. She followed her into the kitchen where her stepmother opened the refrigerator and pulled out a bottle of wine.

Opening it, she poured herself a glass and, without asking, poured another. She set Lorelei's in front of her at the breakfast bar, then walked into the living room to sit down.

For a moment, Lorelei stared at the wine. Then impulsively, she picked it up and downed it before turning her phone to Record and walking into the living room. Even as she did it, she felt as if she was about to betray the woman who'd been her mother. But if Karen had killed that boy...

"I'm at a loss as to what to say to you," Lorelei said as she watched her stepmother sip her wine.

"And yet here you are." There was defiance in her words, in her look.

"You had an affair with Sean Sherman. You destroyed his marriage. Did you also kill his son?" She'd thought her words would get a quick and violent reaction.

Instead, her stepmother took another sip of her wine and set the glass down on the end table next to her before she spoke. "I hate small towns. I told your father that when we moved here. It's like living in a fishbowl." She met Lorelei's gaze. "You were the best part of that marriage. I'd always wanted a child and couldn't have one of my own. I felt like you were my flesh and blood daughter, but I wasn't happy. I loved your father, but he definitely wasn't the love of my life. He couldn't... satisfy me."

"Could anyone?" She regretted the retort at once, sighed and sat down as a long silence fell between them.

"When Fred and I get married, I'm going to put this

house up for sale," Karen said, looking around. "I'll sell the studio as well since we're going to get an apartment in Washington. We'll come here in the summer so it's not like I'm leaving forever, and you can always come visit us in Washington if you want to."

"What about Billy Sherman? You were upset and out driving that night."

Karen got a faraway look in her eye for a moment. "I loved Sean and he loved me. But he was determined to go back to his wife even knowing it would have never worked." She made eye contact again. "Remember when I told you that some women always go for the bad boys?" She chuckled. "That was me. And maybe you since I've seen the look in your eye whenever James Colt's name is mentioned."

"I'm nothing like you," Lorelei said, shaking her head.

Her stepmother chuckled again. "Sean had a wild side."

"What about Fred? Does he have a wild side?"

Karen looked away.

"It's all going to come out," Lorelei said. "Everything. James isn't going to quit, and neither am I."

Her stepmother looked at her again and she saw resignation in Karen's eyes. She felt her heart drop as her stepmother said, "That was one of the worst nights of my life."

When Lorelei spoke, it came out in a whisper. "What did you do?"

Karen took another drink of her wine. "I drove around. I was upset. I wasn't thinking clearly. I was crying and it was raining. I couldn't see anything so I pulled over beside the road. I knew I shouldn't be driving in the condition I was in and yet I couldn't stay in the house with Sean, knowing he was leaving me. My chance of happiness had been snatched away and right or wrong, I blamed Alice."

Lorelei lifted a brow. "After you stole her husband, you blamed her because her husband was going back to her?"

"You can't steal anyone's husband," she snapped with obvious disgust. "That's just what wives say so they don't have to take responsibility for their husbands being unhappy with them."

"I'm sorry, but that sounds like an excuse for what you did," Lorelei said and then quickly waved it away. "I don't care. Are we finally getting to what you did that night?"

"I was sitting in my car crying when this car went by. I heard this *thump-thump* and the brake lights came on and a man jumped out and ran back through the rain. The driver had run over something. I could see a small form lying in the road. The man kicked it off to the edge of the ditch with his boot, ran back and jumped into the car and they drove away."

Lorelei's heart had lodged in her throat. "You saw who killed Billy Sherman?"

"It wasn't Billy. I got out and went over to see. At first I thought it was a dog, then I realized it was a coyote. It was a young one. I picked the poor thing up. It was dead. I don't know where I planned to take it. As I said, I wasn't in my right mind. It doesn't make any sense now, but right then I felt this connection to that dead animal. I started walking down the road holding this dead animal in my arms and crying. I didn't know where I was going or what I was going to do with it."

Lorelei saw the pain in her mother's face, then the anger.

"I decided to leave it on Alice's front doorstep. She was killing me. I wanted her to suffer."

"As if she wasn't suffering enough?"

Karen looked away. "If you'd ever been in love—"

She thought of James and how he'd turned her life upside down. "So you left this dead coyote on her doorstep?"

"That was what I'd planned to do. But as I started by the house I saw her. She was out on her porch having a cigarette. She stubbed it out and went inside, slamming the door. I realized how small and cruel and juvenile my plan was so I turned around and headed back. I can't tell you how badly I felt about all of it, the affair, the people I'd hurt, but most of all the pain in my heart. I wanted so desperately to be loved like I felt I deserved." She glanced at Lorelei. "No offense to your father. He did the best he could, but he—"

"Back to Billy," she said, cutting her off.

Karen nodded. "I hadn't gone very far when I realized there was someone behind me. I turned and…" She swallowed, tears filling her eyes. "It was Billy. He'd been following me."

Chapter Twenty-One

James was headed back into town from the Appleton house when he got the call from Lori. He heard it at once in her voice. "What's wrong?"

"I need to see you." The quaver in her voice sent his pulse rocketing.

"Are you all right?" She had him scared.

"Just meet me at your office, okay?" Her voice broke. "It's important."

"I'm headed there right now," he said and sped up. "Just be careful." But she'd already disconnected.

As he pulled into the alley behind their buildings, she climbed out of her SUV and started toward him. The look on her face made him rush to her and pull her into his arms. She leaned into him for a moment, resting her head on his shoulder, before she pulled back.

He saw the plea in her eyes. Whatever was wrong, she needed to get it out. "Let's go upstairs," he said as he opened the door. He felt a draft, accompanied by a bad feeling. Slowly he began to climb upward, hesitating just before the top to peer down the hallway. Empty. But he could see the door to his office standing open.

Moving closer, he could see that the wood was chewed from where the lock had been jimmied. He wanted to send Lori back to her car. Or into her shop, but he also didn't want to let her out of his sight.

"Stay behind me," he whispered as he pulled his weapon. A cone of light from inside the office shone golden on the hallway floor. He watched it as they moved quietly toward it. But no shadow appeared in the light. No sound of movement came from within the office.

At the door, he motioned Lorelei back for a moment before he burst into the office, his weapon raised and ready to fire. He saw no one and quickly checked the bedroom and bath. Empty.

Turning, he saw Lori framed in the ransacked office doorway. "Who do you think did this?"

"Someone worried about what I've discovered in the case," he said without hesitation as he holstered his gun and, ushering her in, locked the office door and bolted it. Turning to her, he said, "Tell me what's happened. I can see how upset you are."

She reached into her pocket and pulled out her phone. A moment later, he heard Karen Wilkins's voice—and her stepdaughter's.

WHEN THE RECORDING ENDED, Lorelei turned off her phone. At some point, she'd taken the chair James had offered her along with the paper cup of blackberry brandy.

"So, when Billy came face-to-face with your stepmother he screamed and ran into the storm. She didn't go after him. She didn't see him again."

She nodded. "You heard her. She swears it's true. She took the dead coyote into the trees and then she walked back to her car and drove home."

"Billy was killed in the same block from where your stepmother said she'd pulled off the road. I have a witness who saw her car there. Unfortunately, there were no video cameras in that area because of the empty lots and construction going on at the time. The witness killed the coyote just after ten that night. I need to know what time she saw Billy. And what time it was when she returned to her car and where she went after that. She didn't go home until daylight. Sean was at her house waiting for her. He said that she'd fixed her hair and wasn't wet from the storm. So where had she been?"

Lorelei shook her head, drained her blackberry brandy and rose. "I need to go home and try to get some rest. I have to work early tomorrow."

"I'm sorry you got dragged into this," James said as he got to his feet as well. "You look exhausted."

"I am. I knew she was hiding something." She met his gaze. "I honestly don't know what to believe. I thought she and my father had a good marriage. I was wrong about that. I was wrong about so many things. I thought I knew her. Now… I'm not even sure she's telling me the truth. What will you do now?"

"I'll talk to her. I'll tell her what you told me. I won't tell her about the recording. If I can establish a time sequence…"

"You think she did it, don't you?"

"I think she might have blotted it out of her memory. As she said, she wasn't in her right mind. Picking up a dead young coyote and carrying it down the street to play a mean joke? Clearly she wasn't herself."

"But upset enough to run over a little boy on her way home and not remember?" Lorelei shook her head. "We've already established that she's dishonest about at least her love life. We both know there is a part of her story that she's leaving out."

He stepped to her and took her shoulders in his big hands. His touch felt warm and comforting. She wanted to curl up in his arms. "I'm going to find out who killed Billy. Please, I need you to be careful. Someone doesn't want me to know the truth. I doubt they found what they were looking for in my office. I'm afraid of how far they might go to cover up their crime. I don't want you involved."

She smiled sadly. "Too late for that."

"But promise me you won't do any more investigating on your own."

She was too tired and drained and discouraged to argue.

"I'll see you tomorrow?" he said, meeting her gaze.

She nodded numbly and he let her go but insisted on walking her down to her car. He'd wanted to follow her home, except she wasn't having it. It was flattering that James cared, but she wasn't some helpless woman who relied on a man. She wasn't her stepmother. Lorelei wanted a man in her life, but she didn't need one.

"I'm fine," she assured him. "I'm more worried about you."

"Indulge me. Please. Call me when you get home, so I know you made it okay. Promise me?"

JAMES DIDN'T CARE what Lori said. He was going to follow her home to make sure she was safe. He felt as if he'd dragged her into this. Just being associated with him could be bad enough. Add in her stepmother...

As she drove away, he reached for his keys and swore. He'd left them upstairs in his shock at finding his office broken into and ransacked, not to mention the information Lori had gotten on her stepmother.

He turned and rushed upstairs in time to hear his phone ringing. The phone and his keys were on his desk. He scooped up the phone, thinking it might be Lori. It was Gilbert Sanders, the arsonist investigator. He glanced at the time and had a feeling the man wouldn't be calling now unless it was important.

He picked up the call on his way out the door.

"I was thinking about what you said about your father wanting to talk to me about a hit-and-run case he was working on," Gilbert said after a few pleasantries were exchanged. "I couldn't imagine why he'd want to talk to me about anything but a fire. But then I remembered. I *did* talk to him. He told me he was working on a case about a young boy who'd been killed, right?"

"Right. Billy Sherman."

"But that wasn't why your father called me. He wanted to know about a house fire. One fatality. The wife."

James frowned. "Whose fire?"

"His own. Del Colt wanted to know about the fire that killed his wife."

"I don't understand," James said as he reached his pickup and stopped. "My mother died of cancer."

"It was his first wife."

James couldn't speak for a moment. "His *first* wife."

"I'm sorry, you didn't know that your father had been married before?"

"No. What did you tell him about the fire?"

"Just that it had been ruled an accident, a faulty lamp cord. But I wasn't the one who handled that investigation. It was my uncle, the man I was named for, Gilbert T. Sanders, who did the investigation. Your father asked me to look into it for him. Something must have come up in his investigation of the hit-and-run that made him believe the fire that killed his first wife had been arson and was somehow connected to his case."

This made no sense. "Did you look into the fire?" James asked as he climbed into his pickup. Lori would probably be home by now and probably trying to call him.

"I did. I think your father might have been right."

"Wait, right about what?"

"The fire that killed his first wife," Gilbert said. "My uncle suspected it was arson, but there were extenuating circumstances. An eyewitness swore he saw the lamp ignite the living room."

"Who was the eyewitness?"

"Sheriff Otis Osterman. He was the first person on the scene. But I saw in my uncle's notes on the case that there was a string of small fires that summer around Lonesome. There was a suspect at the time."

James felt all the air rush from his lungs as Gilbert said, "Freddie Bayard, now Senator Fred Bayard. Freddie had apparently been a firebug since he was little. But there was no proof and his father, also a senator, made Freddie untouchable. The boy was sent away to a private school where his father promised he would get him the help he needed. In the report, there was also mention of Del and Fred being at odds, some rivalry that went back years."

"How is that possible?" James asked. "I didn't think Fred moved here until about ten years ago."

"His grandparents lived here and he stayed with them more than he stayed with his parents. His father was in DC a lot of the time and he and his mother weren't close. I'm not sure how any of this will help with your investigation."

"Me either, but thank you for letting me know." James pulled in front of Lori's house. No lights on. No Lori. She hadn't come straight home or she would be here by now. Fred Bayard was involved with Karen Wilkins and Lori was involved because of it.

He felt a tremor of fear. Why hadn't Lori gone straight home like she'd planned? Had her stepmother called? Had something happened?

He started to call Lori's cell when he knew where she'd gone. Making a sharp U-turn in the middle of the street, he headed toward her stepmother's house.

As he drove, he couldn't get what Gilbert Sanders had told him out of his mind. He called his brother

Davey only to get voice mail. He tried his brother Tommy. Same thing. He was about to give up when he realized the brother he needed to ask was his eldest brother, Willie.

"What's up?"

"Did you know Dad was married before?" he demanded.

Willie hesitated before saying, "Who told you that?"

"You just did! And you never said anything?" James couldn't believe this.

"Why would I? It had nothing to do with our family," Willie said. "Also, it was too painful for Dad. I wanted to protect him. They were married less than a month when she was killed. Luckily, he met our mom."

"Protect him from what?" James demanded.

"Heartbreak. He blamed himself for her death. Like us, he was on the rodeo circuit all the time. He'd left her alone in a house that had bad wiring. He didn't need to be reminded of the past. That's why I didn't tell you or the others."

"How did you find out?" he asked as he pulled up in front of Lorelei's stepmother's house.

"Otis Osterman told me. He was the cop who investigated the fire. He threw the fact that Dad left his wife in a house with faulty wiring in my face the first time he hauled me in on some trumped-up charge. I told him that if he ever said anything like that to me or my family again, I'd kill him. Apparently, he believed me."

"I'm getting another call," James said, hoping it would be Lori. "We'll talk about this soon." He disconnected from Willie and said, "Lori?"

Silence. He realized that the other call had gone to voice mail. He listened, still hoping it had been Lori. It was one of the out-of-town body shops he'd called inquiring about a vehicle being brought in from Lonesome nine years ago after Billy Sherman's death. He didn't bother to listen to the message. Right now he only cared about Lori. He couldn't shake a bad feeling that she was in trouble.

LORELEI HAD GRUDGINGLY promised to go straight home and call James when she arrived. Her intentions had been good when she'd left him. Until her stepmother called crying and hysterical.

"What's wrong?" Karen didn't answer, just kept crying. "Mom."

Calling her mom seemed to do the trick. "We broke up."

It took Lorelei a minute to realize that she must be talking about the senator.

"Why?"

More awful sobbing, before her stepmother said, "It was all based on a lie. How could I have ever trusted that he was really in love with me? Or that he wasn't just marrying me so I couldn't testify against him?"

At those words, Lorelei felt shaken to her soul. Marry her so she couldn't testify against him? "What are you talking about?"

"That night on the road. Billy." She was sobbing again. "I left out that part. When I was walking back to my car, Fred picked me up. On the way to my car…" More sobbing. "He ran over something in the road. It didn't seem like it was anything. I told him about the coyote… He didn't stop to check but he did look back in his side mirror. I saw his expression. I knew it wasn't a coyote."

Lorelei felt her blood run cold. Her stepmother was sobbing.

"I was so upset and freezing and there didn't seem to be any damage to his vehicle."

"He took you to his house," Lorelei said, seeing now how it had happened with her mother and the senator.

"He was so kind, so caring. I wanted to believe in him." More uncontrollable bawling.

She didn't need her stepmother to tell her what had happened after that night. Fred had been afraid that Karen could come forward with what she knew. He must have seen how much she'd needed a man in her life. He became that man to protect himself. Until Karen finally admitted the truth—and not just about the night Billy Sherman had died.

Lorelei had known women her own age who went from one man to the next, desperate to have someone in their lives. She'd felt sorry for them. She felt sorry for her stepmother. Karen would have been flattered at the senator's attention. She'd been lonely, had needed a man so desperately, that she would rather live a lie than admit the truth about her relationship with Fred Bayard.

Until now.

"You told him what you told me," Lorelei said.

"I knew you were right," her stepmother wailed. "James was going to find out. Fred became so angry. It's over." She began to cry harder.

Why hadn't she noticed how unhappy Karen had been? Why hadn't she known what her stepmother had been going through? Because Karen had seemed happy. And because Lorelei had been busy living her own life, seeing what she wanted to see.

"Mom, I'm almost to your house." But she didn't think Karen heard her. "Mom?" She kept hearing her stepmother's words. *I knew it wasn't a coyote.*

She could hardly make out her stepmother's next words, "Someone's at the back door. It can't be Fred. He's promised to go to the sheriff..." Then Karen's voice changed, and Lorelei knew her stepmother was no longer talking to her. "What are you doing here? I thought—"

Lorelei heard what sounded like the phone being knocked out of Karen's hand. It made a whishing sound as it skittered across the hardwood floor.

She couldn't make out the words, but it sounded like Karen and a man arguing. Then to Lorelei's horror, she heard her stepmother scream followed by a painful cry an instant before she heard the sound of what could be a body hitting the floor.

"Mom?" she cried into the phone. Silence. Then footfalls. The line went dead.

Her hands were shaking so hard on the wheel that she had to grip it tightly. She was calling 911 as her stepmother's house came into view and she saw the smoke.

Chapter Twenty-Two

The smoke seemed to be coming from the back of the house. The man had come in the back door. Lorelei knew who the man was, knew what he'd done and why. But as she made a quick turn and swung down the alley, she was surprised to see him jump into his large dark-colored SUV. She sped toward him as he ducked behind the wheel and took off in a hail of gravel. But not before she'd seen his license plate number. The senator had vanity plates.

She hit her brakes behind the house and bailed out of her vehicle. She could see smoke rolling out of the open back door. She was running toward the house when James came running around the side of the house toward her.

"My stepmother's inside," she screamed over the crackle of the blaze. "The senator was here. I heard him attack her, then set the house on fire." She could see flames rising at the kitchen windows.

"Stay here," James ordered as he pulled off his jean jacket, and putting it over his head ran into the open back door and into the smoke and flames.

Lorelei stood there, feeling helpless. She could hear sirens growing closer. The fire trucks would be here soon. But soon enough? She wanted to race into the house through the smoke and flames and find James, find Karen. She felt her panic building. James was here because of her. He couldn't die because of her.

She began to cry tears of relief as she saw him come out of the smoke carrying Karen. She ran to him as the first of the fire trucks pulled up out front along with an ambulance and the sheriff.

"She's unconscious," James said, coughing. "But since she was on the floor, I don't think she breathed in much smoke."

Lorelei wiped at her tears as she ran to keep up with him as he carried Karen toward the waiting ambulance. James had risked his life to save her stepmother. She loved this man. The thought whizzed through her mind as they reached the sidewalk and were immediately surrounded by frantic activity as James handed over Karen and the EMTs went to work on her.

"Want to tell me what's going on here?" the sheriff asked as he sauntered up to Lorelei.

"My stepmother was attacked and left in a burning house to die," she snapped. "That's what happened. I saw the man who assaulted her and started the fire. I was on the phone with her when he attacked her. I was only a block away so I saw him running away as I drove up. I took down his license number. But I also saw his face. It was Senator Fred Bayard."

Carl started to argue that she had to be mistaken.

"Fred is a godsend to this community. Without him and the donations he'd made—"

Karen, now conscious, pulled off her oxygen mask. She narrowed her gaze on the sheriff, stopping the EMTs from loading her gurney into the back of the ambulance.

"Senator Fred Bayard tried to kill me and then he set my house on fire," her stepmother said through coughing fits. "He also killed Billy Sherman. I know because I was in the car with him. He didn't stop to see what he'd run over. He just kept going. He would have killed me too."

The EMTs got the oxygen back on Karen as she gasped for breath.

"If you don't arrest the senator," Lorelei said, turning to the sheriff, "I will call the FBI and tell them that you refused to pick up the man who assaulted my stepmother, started the fire and left her to die. I don't think you want them looking into the other things you and your brother have done over the years to cover up crimes in Lonesome."

The EMTs loaded Karen into the ambulance. "I have to get to the hospital," she said and pushed past the sheriff.

"I'll take you," James said, suddenly at her side. He put his arm around her as they hurried to his pickup. She leaned into him, for once happy to have someone to lean on.

As she climbed in and he slid behind the wheel, she told him what her stepmother had told her on the phone before she'd heard Karen being attacked.

"When I drove up, I saw him running from the back of the house," she said. "He tried to kill my stepmother to cover up his crime." She fought tears, fearing that Fred would get away with it. The sheriff certainly didn't have the guts to arrest him.

Sheriff Carl Osterman swore as he watched the ambulance leave, siren blaring and lights flashing. James Colt and Lorelei Wilkins took off behind it. When had those two become so tight, he wondered. He'd thought Lorelei had more sense. Shaking his head, he watched the firefighters trying to put out the blaze and then sighing, climbed into his patrol SUV and headed out to the senator's place.

He knew how this was going to go down so he was in no hurry. It would come down to the senator's word against the woman he'd just broken up with and Lorelei, a younger woman protecting her stepmother. Not the best witnesses especially if all this had been caused by a domestic disagreement between the senator and Karen Wilkins. He certainly didn't want to take the word of a hysterical woman.

As he pulled up in the yard in front of the large summer house, he slowly got out. He wasn't surprised when Fred came out carrying a small suitcase and walked toward his helipad next to the house in a clearing in the pines.

Carl followed him. "If you have a minute, Fred?"

"Sheriff, good to see you. Actually, I don't. Something's come up. My chopper should be here any minute. I need to get to the airport. Government business."

The senator smelled as if he'd taken a quick shower, so quick that there was still that faint hint of smoke on him. "We have a problem," Carl said.

Fred smiled. "I'm sure it's nothing that you can't handle, Sheriff. It's one of the reasons I backed your campaign. Please don't tell me I supported the wrong man."

He could hear the sound of the helicopter in the distance. "You did back the right man," Carl said, bristling. "But money can only buy so much. This time I'm going to have to take you in for questioning, Fred. Lorelei Wilkins saw you leaving her stepmother's house. You stepped over a line. What you did can't be undone."

The senator shook his head. "I was at her house. I'm not sure what happened after I left, but I had just broken up with her stepmother. Karen was overwrought, threatening to kill herself. Of course Lorelei is going to blame me if the woman did something…stupid."

"It's more serious than that, I'm afraid, Fred. Karen regained consciousness. She says you assaulted her and set her house on fire. Lorelei was on a phone call with her stepmother and heard it all. Karen also says that you killed Billy Sherman—that she was in the car that night and will testify in court that you didn't even stop."

"She's lying. I told you. I broke it off. She'd say anything to get back at me." The helicopter came into view.

Carl pulled out his handcuffs. A part of him had known that this day was coming and had been for years. Fred had gotten away with numerous crimes over the years since he was a boy. Back then he'd been a juvenile, his father a respected senator, his grandparents churchgoing people. But now that the man's house of cards had started to tumble, the sheriff suspected a lot more was about to come out.

Worse, Carl knew that he and Otis would be caught in the dirt once it started flying. He laid his hand on his weapon and slowly unsnapped the holster. Fred saw the movement, his eyes widening. The senator had to know that there was an easy way out of this for Carl, for his brother. If Fred were dead there would never be a trial, a lot of old cases wouldn't come to light.

"I hope you'll come peacefully, senator," Carl said. "But either way, you're going to have to come down to the station for questioning." He met the man's gaze and held it for a long moment.

Fred swore. "All the things I've done for your two-bit town." He angrily pulled out his phone and called his attorney.

"I'll tell the helicopter pilot that you won't be going anywhere for a while," Carl said, then turned back to the senator. "By the way, I heard from Gilbert Sanders, the state arson investigator, earlier today. He told me that he's reopening the Del Colt fire case. He thinks he has some new evidence." He watched Fred's spray-on-tanned face pale. "He was especially interested in talking to you."

"The statute of limitations on arson is five years."

"I guess you forgot. Del's first wife died in that fire. There is no statute of limitations on murder."

Chapter Twenty-Three

Lorelei found her stepmother to be in good spirits when she stopped by the hospital the next morning. Karen had a concussion from the blow the senator had dealt her and a mild cough from the smoke, but she was going to be fine.

"The prosecutor said he didn't think I would be arrested for withholding evidence," Karen said. "I'm just glad to be alive. But I can't stay in Lonesome. I should have left a long time ago."

She took her stepmother's hand. "You stayed because of me."

Karen smiled. "You always did give me the benefit of the doubt. I will miss you, but you need to get on with your life. You need not worry about me anymore."

She wasn't sure about that. "You put up the money for my shop from your retirement account."

"It was the right thing to do. I inherited the house and your father's money. It's what your father would have wanted me to do."

"I'm sorry things didn't work out for you," Lorelei said.

"I chose the wrong men for the wrong reasons." She

shook her head. "I've learned my lesson. Don't look at me like that. Even old dogs can learn new tricks."

Lorelei laughed. "You're still young. There's someone out there for you."

"I hope so." She took a ragged breath. "What's going on with you and James Colt?"

She shrugged. "We had a moment, but now he's done what he set out to do. Solve his father's case. I'm sure he'll be going back on the rodeo circuit."

"I'm sorry."

"I'm sure it's for the best," Lorelei said. "I heard you're getting out of here today."

"I'm thinking of going to Chicago. I'll be back for the trial, if Fred's case goes to trial. But first I have to tie up some loose ends with the insurance company and the house. I've had an offer for the exercise studio and I've decided to take it. I'm looking forward to a fresh start in the big city."

She squeezed her stepmother's hand. "Please keep in touch."

"You know I will. You're my daughter." They hugged and Lorelei left before she cried. She would miss Karen. Her stepmother had been the last link she had with her father and the last reminder of her childhood. With Karen gone, she had no family left here.

The thought made her sad as she drove to her shop. Anita had volunteered to come in and work, which Lorelei had happily accepted. Given everything that had happened, she needed a little time off. Karen thought she was like her because of James Colt. Was he her bad boy? He had played that part in high school and for some time after, but she no longer thought of him that way. He was her hero. But he was also a rodeo cowboy at heart. The circuit would be calling him now.

As she got out of her SUV, James drove up. Just seeing him made her heart soar. Yesterday evening he'd gone to the hospital with her, but she'd sent him home after the doctors checked him over. He had smoke inhalation and she could tell he needed rest. He'd called to make sure she and Karen were both all right late last night. She hadn't had a chance to talk to him since.

He got out of his pickup and sauntered toward her. Had she really not noticed how good-looking he was that first day when she'd seen him again after all the years? She could laugh about it now. She'd thought his hair was too long, that he dressed like a saddle tramp, that he was too arrogant for a man who obviously lacked ambition. So why did he seem perfect now? He hadn't changed, but the way she saw him definitely had, she realized. She'd gotten to know the man inside him and fallen in love with him.

The thought struck her at heart level like a blow. She'd had the thought yesterday after he'd gone into a house on fire to save her stepmother. This time the thought carried no raw emotion. It just happened to be the truth.

And now he would be leaving Lonesome, leaving her.

"I'm starved," he said, grinning as he joined her.

"You're always starved," she said with a laugh.

He put his arm around her as they headed into the

back of her sandwich shop. He did it casually and yet it sent a jolt through her. "What's the special today?"

"Pulled pork. Your favorite."

He looked over at her and smiled. "You know me so well. Anita must be working. Thank goodness since I don't want you going anywhere near my sandwich."

She thought of that day when she'd added hot sauce and sliced jalapeños to his sandwich—and he'd eaten every bite of it. "I'm still sorry about that."

"Sure you are," he said with a laugh as he headed for his usual table. "Have an early lunch with me?"

Lorelei nodded, fighting tears. She didn't want to think about the days he would no longer stop by. When his pickup wouldn't be parked in the alley next door. When she wouldn't see him. "Let me place our orders. I'll be right back. Iced tea or lemonade?"

"Both." He looked so happy. He'd solved his father's last case. Why wouldn't he be happy? But she feared it was more about going back on the rodeo circuit.

JAMES TOOK HIS usual seat at the booth and looked out on the town. Funny how his attitude toward Lonesome had changed. It had been nothing more than a stopover on his way somewhere else for so many years. He realized that he hadn't appreciated it.

Now he felt more a part of the place. It was a good feeling, one he would miss if...when he went back on the rodeo circuit. He'd done what he'd set out to do. Solve his father's last case. Still, it felt unfinished. There was the question of his father's death. He thought the truth about it still might come out—if as he suspected Otis had something to do with Del Colt's death.

The senator's arrest had a domino effect. The feds had stepped in and taken over the case. Gilbert Sanders turned over new evidence to the prosecutor regarding the Del Colt case along with other fires that were quickly attributed to Fred. He was being held without bail.

A small-time criminal Otis Osterman had arrested back when he was sheriff was picked up and charged for drug possession. He copped a plea, giving up Otis as the one who'd hired him to burn down Cora Brooks's house. The prosecution, closely watched by the feds, began looking into how other investigations had been handled by both Carl Osterman and his brother Otis. Under pressure, Carl had resigned, and the reign of the Osterman's was over. More of their misdeeds would be coming out, James knew.

He dragged himself out of his thoughts as Lori appeared with a tray full of food and drinks. "I'm sorry. I could have helped you with that."

She gave him a dismissive look. "I do this for a living. I can handle it."

He watched her slide into the chair across from him and take everything off the tray. He'd never imagined he would have these kinds of feelings for Lorelei Wilkins and yet he did. Once, it had been flirting. Now... Now it was so much more. She had a pull on him stronger than gravity.

"What will happen now with the case?" she asked

after they'd tucked into their sandwiches in companionable silence.

"Probably the most Fred will go down for will be assault, arson and manslaughter even if the prosecution can prove he set the fire that killed my father's first wife. He might get some time in prison, but probably not much. But his career is over. He'll be a felon. He won't even be allowed to vote, own a gun or hold office in most states and there are countries that won't allow him in."

She put down her sandwich. "It's not enough. What about Billy?"

James shook his head. "I doubt a jury will convict him on that because of lack of evidence. Karen says he ran over something. All Fred has to do is lie and say he didn't. It's her word against his. There apparently wasn't any damage to his large SUV."

"He's in a position where he can lie and there will be people who will believe him over my stepmother."

James couldn't argue that. "Taking away his career and ruining his reputation will hurt the most. He'll lie, say he was railroaded by a scorned woman. That he was innocent of all of it. But he ran from your stepmother's house after assaulting her and setting her house on fire. Add to that the other fires… His reputation is toast."

He watched her pick at her sandwich as if she'd lost her appetite. "Do you think he would have married Karen?"

She shook her head. "I think she realized there was no happy ending with the lie between them. She would have always questioned his love for her."

James reached across the table to cover her hand with his own. "People disappoint us but ultimately we're all human. That's what my dad used to say. We do what we have to do to survive. For some, that's lying, cheating, stealing and even killing. For others it's small lies and secrets. My dad was good at uncovering them and finding a little justice or at least peace for those in pain. I understand now why he loved doing this."

"So you're hooked on the PI business?" She'd said it jokingly, but he knew at the heart of her question what she was asking. This year's rodeo season was in full swing. He was healed. There was nothing to keep him from getting back to his life. He'd accomplished what he'd set out to do. Solve his father's last case—with Lori's help. If he didn't go soon...

Lori. He looked into her face, saw her compassion, her spirit, her desire that mirrored his own. How could he leave her for months to go back on the rodeo circuit? But then how could he not? He wasn't getting any younger. He didn't have that much time left in the saddle and there were a lot of broncos he'd yet to ride.

LORELEI STOOD IN the kitchen of her shop after James left. He'd said there were some things he had to take care of and that he would see her later. She and her friend Anita were prepping for the next day and getting ready for the lunch crowd. It was Saturday and a beautiful summer day. There would be a lot of picnickers coming for her special weekend basket.

"I keep thinking about everything that happened,"

she said, voicing her doubts out loud. "It doesn't feel over."

"I'm sure it's going to take a while to process everything." She and Anita had been good friends in high school. While Lorelei had gone to college, Anita had married her childhood sweetheart, had babies and settled in Lonesome. Lorelei looked up to her since Anita had definitely had more life experience because of it.

"I keep thinking about something Karen said. She heard a car go by moving fast when she was in the trees getting rid of the coyote. She hid, so she didn't see the car or the driver. She said that's when she realized that she couldn't do what she'd been doing anymore. That she needed to find a man who appreciated her and wanted to marry her and that things were really over between her and Sean."

Anita stopped to plant one hand on her hip. "Where are you going with this?"

"I'm not sure. Right after that, she stepped back on the highway in the pouring rain and was picked up by the senator," Lorelei said. "Of course, Karen thought it was fate."

"Until the senator hit Billy."

"That's just it. Karen said he ran over *something* in the road. Not that he *hit* something."

"I'm not sure I see the difference."

"That car that sped by too fast while Karen was hiding in the trees, what if that's the driver who actually hit and killed Billy Sherman?"

"But you don't know who it was."

"No. Minutes later the senator would pick up Karen

and run over something in the road and not bother to stop." She grimaced. "He must have seen the boy lying on the road in his rearview mirror."

"Well, you know what kind of man he is already," Anita said.

"But what if Billy was already dead? What if the senator panicked, thinking he had killed the boy and believing Karen would know he'd done it? When he looked back in his side mirror, he would have seen the boy's clothing. From that moment on, he had to keep my stepmother from ever telling so he seduced her that night."

Anita shuddered. "And when he realized he could no longer trust her, he tried to kill her and burn down her house."

"Maybe that's what he planned all along. I really doubt he would have married her and yet he couldn't break up with her for fear of what she might do. He must have felt trapped. How ironic would it be if he was innocent?"

"Innocent is not a word I would use with him, but I see what you mean," Anita agreed. "But how can you prove that Billy was already dead, hit by the car before the senator's vehicle drove over the remains?"

"I have no idea," Lorelei said. "But I'm going by Alice Sherman's today. My stepmother was going to stop by her house, but I talked her out of it. Karen wanted to send her a card to tell her how sorry she was about everything. She's now decided that to change she needs to apologize to those she hurt."

"Not a bad idea."

"No, but I think Karen showing up there might not

be a great idea. So I said I'd drop off the card she wrote instead. I wanted to see if Alice might remember a car flying past that night. My stepmother said Alice had been outside smoking a cigarette when she'd seen her but had gone back inside. I would imagine she'd been at the window making sure Karen kept going past."

Anita looked skeptical. "Are you sure she'll want to talk to you? I mean, you are Karen's daughter. But what's the worst that can happen? She'll throw you out."

"That's a pleasant thought," she said as she tossed her apron in the bin and headed for her SUV parked outside. But she had to try.

She noticed that James's pickup was still parked in the alley. She considered sharing her theory with him but decided otherwise. There was a good chance that the senator had been the one to hit Billy in that big SUV of his with the huge metal guard on the front. Questioning Alice Sherman probably wouldn't go anywhere anyway.

On top of that, she could see a shadow moving around in the upstairs apartment. Was James packing? Would he tell her goodbye?

JAMES HAD LOOKED around the office, his gaze lighting on his private investigator's license. He'd taken Lori's advice. He'd framed it and put it on the wall next to his father's. It had felt presumptuous. But he liked the look of it there.

He knew he should start packing. He needed to pick up his horse and trailer. He turned and saw the Colt Investigations sign in the front second-story window. He should take that down. He'd already had several calls from people wanting to hire him as the news had swept through Lonesome.

The crazy part was that he would never have solved it without Lori's help. He still didn't know what he was doing. He was playacting at being a PI. But it had given him some experience. Maybe with more...

The worst part was that something was still nagging at him about the case. He told himself that the FBI would get to the bottom of any questions he might have. Everything was in good hands.

He turned to look at his framed PI license hanging on the wall over the desk next to his father's again. He felt torn about leaving. When he thought about Lori he wasn't sure he could leave. But would he regret it later if he didn't go at least one more year on the circuit? It would probably be his last.

His cell phone rang. "Congrats," Willie said. "You're all over the news. Dad would be proud."

"Thanks."

"I suppose I know what you're doing. Packing. Did I hear you might catch up to us in Texas?"

"Thinking about it."

"What? You aren't already packed? What's going on?" James knew he had to make a decision. He still didn't know how or why his father had died that night on the railroad tracks. He feared that he never would.

He'd been offered more cases since the senator's arrest. Maybe he could make a living at this PI thing. He and Lori had found Billy Sherman's killer. They'd made a good team.

"I'm packing," he told his brother. "I'll let you know,

but probably Texas." He disconnected. But something was still nagging him. About the case? About leaving?

He stepped over to the desk and sat down. Earlier, he'd filed the case away. Now he pulled it out. There were his own notes in with his father's. Would his father be proud?

What was bothering him? He flipped through the file, stopping on the coroner's report. He'd read it over when he'd first started the case. Billy's injuries had been consistent with being hit by a vehicle. Numerous bones had been broken but it was a massive head injury that was listed as cause of death.

Numerous bones had been broken, he read again and looked through the list. Billy's right arm had been shattered and was believed to have been run over by the vehicle's tire after initial impact.

He picked up his phone and called Dr. Milton Stanley. He figured the man would be out working in his yard and was surprised when he picked up. "This is a bit unusual, but I was looking at the coroner's report on Billy Sherman. I need to know if this is consistent with a small boy of seven being struck by a large vehicle."

"It would depend on the size of the car. If it was a large SUV or pickup or a small car, the injuries would be different. The state medical examiner did this autopsy. Send me the report and I'd be happy to give you my opinion."

James glanced around the office and spotted his father's old fax machine. "I can fax it to you. I don't have a copy machine."

The doctor laughed. "How about a computer? No?

If you're going to stay in business, son, you need to get into at least the twentieth century. Just take a photo of it with your phone and send it to me."

He'd just hung up, wondering what it was he was looking for when his cell phone rang. When he saw it was one of the out-of-town body shops he'd called, he remembered that one of them had called him back but he'd never listened to the message or returned the call. He'd forgotten about it with everything else that had been going on.

"You still looking for a vehicle that might have been involved in a hit-and-run?" a man asked.

He wasn't and yet he heard himself say, "What do you have?"

"I saw the message you left about looking for a damaged vehicle after April 10th nine years ago. I killed the message before my boss saw it," the man said. "Otherwise, no one would be calling you right now."

Did the man want money? Was that what this was about? "So why are you calling me?"

"After that date you mentioned, we had a car come in. It was late at night on a lowboy trailer. My boss had it dumped off. He pushed it into one of the bays. He didn't know I was still in the garage. I was curious so after he left I took a look at it. It wasn't the first car that rolled in that was…questionable. This one bothered me because there was blood on it and…hair."

Even as James told himself that this wasn't Billy's hit-and-run, he felt his heart plummet. This vehicle had been involved in a hit-and-run somewhere. Unless this guy was just leading him on. "Why didn't you report it?"

"My boss was an ass but I needed the job. My old lady was pregnant."

"You don't work there anymore?" He waited for the man to ask for money.

"I won't after this. I was suspicious so I bagged the hair and a scrap of clothing that was stuck in the bumper. Now I find out that the clothing matched the description of what that boy was wearing. I also took a piece of clean cloth and I wiped up some of the blood and put it into the bag for insurance. Look, I could get in trouble for this in so many ways. But now I've got a kid and when I heard about the trial of that senator for running over that boy... I want to see him hang."

So did James. "The FBI is going to want that bag with the evidence in it and your statement. Will you do it?"

Silence, then finally, "What the hell. My old lady says it's bad karma if I don't. It's been bothering me for the past nine years."

"They'll also want the make and model of the car."

"No problem. I even took down the license plate number." He rattled it off and James wrote it down. He was frowning down at what he'd written, when the man said, "It was a mid-sized sedan. I took a photo. Hold on, I'll send it to you."

A few moments later, the photo appeared on James's phone. By then he knew deep down what he'd been fearing. The car wasn't Senator Fred Bayard's large black SUV. The license plate number had been wrong as well.

Heart in his throat, he stared at the car in the photo and remembered where he'd seen it. Parked in front of Alice Sherman's house.

Chapter Twenty-Four

Lorelei was about to give up. After ringing the doorbell several times and finally knocking at Alice Sherman's door, she still hadn't been able to raise anyone. She'd seen the car in the garage so she suspected the woman was home. There had been a news van parked outside when Lorelei had driven up, but it left after she hadn't gotten an answer at the door.

She was about to leave the card from her stepmother when the door opened a crack.

"What do you want?" Alice wore a bathrobe and slippers. Her hair looked as if it hadn't been washed in days. The woman stared at her, clearly not having a clue who she was.

"Mrs. Sherman, I'm—"

"It's not 'Mrs.' You're a local. I've seen you before. You one of those reporters?"

"No," she quickly assured her before the woman could close the door. "I'm Lorelei Wilkins. I own the sandwich shop in town. I just stopped by to—"

"Wilkins?" She grabbed hold of the door as if she needed it for support. "You're related to Karen?"

"She's my stepmother. She's in the hospital—"

"Like I care." Tears welled in Alice's eyes. "I hate her. I hope she dies."

"I'm sorry." Lorelei was still holding the card in her hand.

"What's that?"

"It's a note from my...from Karen."

Alice's eyes widened. "She sent you with a card for me? How thoughtful after what she did to my life," she said, her voice filled with rancor. Suddenly the woman opened the door wider. "You should come in."

That had been her hope originally, using the card as an excuse. But now she wasn't so sure. "I don't want to disturb you—"

"Too late for that. Come in."

Lorelei hesitated for a moment before stepping in. As she did, Alice Sherman snatched the card from her hand.

"Sit." She tore into the envelope. "Did she tell you what she did to me?" Alice didn't wait for an answer. "She destroyed my life and now everyone is going to know and she and her boyfriend are going to pay. It's just too bad my ex-husband isn't going to prison too."

"The senator's not her boyfriend anymore," Lorelei said as Alice motioned her into a chair. This was clearly not the best time to be asking questions about Billy's death, she thought. But then again she couldn't imagine a time that would be. The senator's arrest and Karen's part in it had obviously opened the old wounds— wounds Lorelei suspected hadn't ever started to heal.

"But he *was* her boyfriend," Alice said, showing that she had been listening. "Karen lied to protect him and herself after they killed my boy."

Lorelei took a seat. She watched her read the card not once, but twice before she ripped it up and threw it into the fireplace.

Alice reached into a container on the hearth, drew out a match, struck it and tossed it into the shredded paper. Flames licked through the card in a matter of seconds before dying out.

"What did you really come over here for?" Alice asked, turning to face her. "It wasn't to bring me a card from your mother."

She didn't correct her. She thought of Karen as her mother. "You're right. I had wanted to ask you about the night Billy died."

Alice looked surprised. "Why? The cops have Billy's killers."

"I was hoping you could help me with something. Karen was in the pines not too far from here when she heard a car go racing past."

The woman's eyes narrowed. "The senator."

Lorelei shook her head. "He didn't drive by until minutes later when Karen was walking back up the road toward her car. I was wondering if you saw the vehicle go by? If you might have recognized it."

"I had other things on my mind besides looking out the window."

She couldn't help her surprise or hide it. Alice was looking at her expectantly, waiting as if almost daring Lorelei to call her a liar. "It's just that you saw my stepmother."

"I don't know what you're talking about." Alice rubbed the back of her neck as she turned to look at the ashes in the fireplace, her back to Lorelei.

"My mother had been headed for your house but when she saw you and when you saw her, she changed her mind."

Alice picked up the poker and began jabbing at the charred remains of the card lying in the bottom of the fireplace. "I just told you I didn't look out the window."

Lorelei felt a chill move slowly up her spine. One of them was lying and this time, she believed it wasn't Karen. A thought struck her as she watched the woman's agitation increasing with each jab of the poker. "She said you quickly disappeared from the window. Not long after that, she heard the car go racing by." The chill moved through her, sending a wave of goose bumps over her flesh.

In that instant, she knew. Worse, Alice knew that she'd put it together. Lorelei shot to her feet, but not quickly enough. Alice spun around, the poker in her hand, getting between Lorelei and the door.

Brandishing the poker, the woman began to make a wailing sound. Lorelei took a step back and then another as she shoved her hand into her pocket for her phone and looked for a way out.

The wailing stopped as abruptly as it had started. Alice got a distant look in her eyes that was more frightening than the wailing. "I saw her out there through the rain. She'd taken my husband, destroyed my family. I knew Sean had broken it off with her. I knew that was why she was out there in the rain. I hated her. I just wanted her dead. Then I saw her turn and head back up the road toward her house."

Lorelei felt her phone in her pocket, but she didn't dare draw it out as Alice advanced on her, brandishing the poker.

"I went into the garage and got into my car. I opened the garage door, hoping it wouldn't wake Billy. I planned to be gone for only a few minutes. I knew exactly what I had to do. She'd asked for it and now she was going to get what she had coming to her."

Lorelei bumped into the kitchen table. She glanced toward the back door, but knew she'd never reach it in time. Alice stopped a few feet away. Her eyes looked glazed over as if lost in the past, but Lorelei didn't dare move as she took in her surroundings—looking for something she could use for a weapon.

When Alice spoke, her voice had taken on a sleep-walking kind of sound effect. "It was raining so hard, the night was so dark. I saw the figure running down the road. I hit the gas going faster and faster. The rain was coming down so hard, the wipers were beating frantically and…" Alice stopped talking, her eyes wide with horror. She began to cry. "I didn't know. How could I know? It was so dark, the rain… I didn't know." The poker wavered in her hands. "What was he doing out there in the storm? I thought he was in bed. I thought…" She looked at Lorelei, her gaze focusing and then hardening as her survival instincts took over. "I thought I killed Karen. She took my husband and then my son.

"And now I'm going to take her daughter."

Lorelei's cell began to ring, startling them both.

JAMES TRIED LORELEI'S cell on his way over to Alice's. At lunch, he remembered their discussion. Something had been nagging at Lori too, he realized. The same thing that had been bothering him.

Karen had said that the senator ran over something. Not hit something. That had been the clue the whole time. When the call to Lori went to voice mail, he called Karen. She said she'd just gotten home from the hospital after being released.

"Have you see Lorelei?" he asked, trying not to sound as worried as he was.

"She was going over to Alice Sherman's house. I had a card I wanted her to deliver."

James swore. "Call 911 and tell them to get over there. I'm on my way. Lorelei could be in trouble."

He sped toward Alice Sherman's house. He remembered Karen saying that she'd heard a car go racing past while she was in the pines getting rid of the coyote. That was after seeing Alice—and after Alice saw her walking down the road in the rainstorm. He desperately wanted to be wrong.

Just the thought of what Alice might have done, what she'd been living with… If he was right, she'd killed her own son and then covered it up. What would she do if forced to face what she'd done? That was what terrified him. If Lorelei asked too many questions…

He was almost to Alice's house. He could see Lori's car parked in the driveway. He just prayed he was wrong, but all his instincts told him that she was in trouble. He just prayed he could reach her in time.

Chapter Twenty-Five

Alice ran at her, swinging the poker, aiming for her head. Lorelei had only a second to react. She grabbed the back of the wooden chair next to her at the table and heaved it at the woman. The chair legs struck the poker, knocking it out of Alice's hands and forcing her back. The poker clattered to the kitchen floor and then skittered toward the refrigerator away from both of them.

Shoving the fallen chair aside, Alice came at her like something feral. "You and your boyfriend just couldn't leave it alone. Billy is buried. Why can't you let him rest in peace?"

"Alice, you don't want to do this," Lorelei cried as she managed to get on the other side of the kitchen table. "It was an accident. You didn't know it was Billy."

But the woman was shaking her head as she suddenly veered to the right. She thought Alice was going for the poker on the floor in front of the refrigerator deeper in the kitchen. She decided to make a run for it. She had just come around the end of the table and was headed for the living room and the front door beyond it at a run when she heard the gunshot. Sheetrock dust and particles fell over her, startling her as much as the loud report of the gun.

"Take another step and the next bullet will be for you," Alice cried.

Lorelei turned slowly to look back. The woman held the gun in both hands, her stance a warning that she was no novice at this.

"We're going to go for a ride," Alice said and motioned with the gun toward the door to the garage.

Lorelei had seen enough movies and read enough thrillers to know that you never wanted to be taken to a second location. That was where someone would eventually stumble over your shallow grave. Or their dog would dig up your remains. It was how you made the headlines.

But she also thought that as desperate as Alice appeared, maybe she should take her chances. From the look in the woman's eyes, she would shoot her here and now—just as she'd warned. Maybe during the drive Lorelei might see an opportunity to get the upper hand.

Out in the garage, Alice ordered her behind the wheel. As she climbed in, Alice got in the other side and ordered, "Start the car. I will shoot you if you do anything but what I tell you."

The key was in the ignition. As Alice hit the garage door opener, Lorelei snapped on her seatbelt, started the car and drove out of the garage.

"Go left."

She turned onto the street, her brain whirling. So far Alice hadn't buckled up. Lorelei was debating what to do when she saw James's pickup racing up the other side of the street. She swerved in front of him hoping to get his attention.

"What do you think you're doing?" Alice demanded, shoving the gun into her face as they sped past James. Had he seen her? Had he seen Alice and the gun pointed at her head?

"You called him!" Alice screamed. "I told you not to do anything stupid, but you did." She had turned in the seat and was looking back.

In her rearview mirror, Lorelei saw James make a U-turn and come after them. He had seen her, but Lorelei realized it had been a mistake to draw his attention. James couldn't save her. Alice would kill her before that.

Worse, Alice had put down her window and was now shooting at James. In the rearview mirror, she saw the pickup's windshield shatter.

Lorelei swerved back and forth as she tried to keep the woman from getting a clean shot at James. He'd knocked out the rest of the windshield and was still coming up fast behind them. She swerved again and Alice banged her head on the window frame.

"You silly fool," the woman screeched, turning the gun on her. "I told you. Didn't I tell you? You've left me no choice."

Lorelei hit the gas again. She knew she had to act fast. Alice was too close to the edge. It would be just like her to pull the trigger and then turn the gun on herself. She slammed her foot down hard on the gas. The car jumped forward, the speed climbing quickly.

"What are you doing?" Alice cried. They were on the straightaway almost to the spot where Billy had died.

Alice was screaming as if she'd realized where they were. "No! No!" She took aim and Lorelei knew what she had to do.

Keeping the gas pedal to the floor, she suddenly swerved to the right. The car bounced down into the shallow ditch. Alice, still not belted in, was slammed against the door, throwing her off balance in the seat as she tried to aim the gun at her.

But Lorelei didn't let up on the gas as she pointed the vehicle toward the stand of pines in the empty lot across from where Billy died.

"I should have killed you at the house!" Alice screamed as she took aim at Lorelei's head.

The car bucking and bouncing across the field, she let go of the steering wheel with one hand to try to grab for the gun. The shot was deafening, but nothing like the sound when the car hit the trees.

JAMES COULDN'T BELIEVE what he was seeing. He'd never felt more helpless as he watched Alice's car leave the road. It roared down into the ditch then headed for the pines. He hit his brakes, barely getting his pickup stopped before the car crashed into the pines.

He leaped out and ran toward the wrecked car. Steam rose from the engine. He could see that the front end of the car was badly damaged—mostly on the passenger side. Lori had been behind the wheel. As he raced to that side, Connie Matthews came out of her house.

"Call 911. Hurry!" he yelled at her as he reached the

driver's side door and saw that the window had been shot out. He felt his heart drop. Had Alice shot her? Is that why the car had left the road, why it had crashed into the pines?

Inside he could see Lori. Her airbag had gone off and was now deflated over the steering wheel with Lori draped over it. There was blood dripping onto the deflated airbag.

He noticed it all in a split second as he tried unsuccessfully to open her door. Past her, he could see Alice. She'd gone through the windshield and now lay partly sprawled across the hood. She hadn't been wearing her seatbelt. Nor had her airbag activated.

James could hear sirens headed their way. He put all his weight into opening the door, surprised when he looked down and noticed his own blood. He'd taken a bullet in his arm but hadn't even realized it.

The door groaned and finally gave. In an instant he was at Lori's side. He felt for a pulse, terrified he wouldn't find one. There it was. Strong, just like her. He felt tears burn his eyes as relief rushed over him.

"Lori?" he said as he knelt beside the car. "It's going to be all right, baby. It's all going to be all right now. You're a fighter. Don't leave me. Please, don't leave me."

Soon he heard the EMTs coming, telling him to step aside. He rose and moved away, running a hand over his face as he watched them go to work. One of the EMTs noticed he was bleeding and pulled him aside.

More sirens and more rigs pulled up. Workers rushed past with a gurney for Lori. He turned away as he saw them checking Alice. It had been clear right away that she was gone.

He didn't remember going back to his pickup and following the ambulance to the hospital. Just as he didn't remember calling his brothers. Just as he didn't remember the doctors taking care of his gunshot wound or giving his statement to a law enforcement officer. All he'd thought about was Lori.

Hours later, he was walking the floor in the waiting room, when Willie arrived, followed soon after by Davey and Tommy. The surgeon had come in shortly after that to tell him that Lori had survived and was in stable condition.

"You should go on home and get some rest," the doctor told him. "You won't be able to see her until later today anyway."

He hadn't wanted to leave, but his brothers had taken him under their capable wings. When he'd awakened hours later in his bed, he'd gotten up to find them sitting in their dad's office. His arm ached. He'd looked down at the bandage, the horror of what had happened coming back to him.

"I just called the hospital," Willie said as James walked into the room. "I talked to a nurse I know. Lorelei's good. If she keeps improving as she has, you can see her later today."

James's knees felt weak with relief as he dropped into his father's office chair his brother Tommy had vacated for him.

"Now tell us what the hell has been going on here," Willie said. "Tommy went out to get us something to eat and came back with newspapers. You're a famous detective?"

"Not quite or Lori wouldn't be in the hospital right now," he said.

"Lori, is it?" Willie asked, grinning. "We saved you something to eat and made coffee. You fixed up the place pretty nice. But I think you'd better tell us what's been going on."

When he finished telling them between bites of breakfast washed down by coffee and a pain pill, his brothers were staring at him.

"You're good at this?" Davey said and laughed.

"Not quite," he said. "I almost got myself and Lori killed."

"You solved the case," Willie said.

James shook his head. "I almost got Lori killed."

"It's pretty clear to me what's going on here," Davey said. "James is in love."

His three brothers looked at him as if waiting for him to deny it. But he couldn't. It was true. He loved Lori. He repeated it out loud. "I love Lori."

His brothers all laughed, stealing glances at each other as if they couldn't believe it. James was the last one they'd have expected to get serious about anyone.

"Wait, what are you saying? You're giving up rodeo?" Tommy said.

Lori opened her eyes and blinked. She thought she was seeing double. No, not double, quadruple. Four men dressed in Western attire standing at the end of her bed. All tall, dark and handsome as sin. One in particular caught her eye. She smiled at James and closed her eyes again.

When she woke up again, James was sitting by her bed. "I dreamed that there were four of you," she said, her hoarse voice sounding strange to her. "Four handsome cowboys."

He rose quickly to take her hand. "My brothers."

"I haven't seen them in years. They're…gorgeous."

James grinned down at her. "You're still drugged up, aren't you."

She nodded, smiling. "I can't feel anything but this one spot on my head." She reached up to touch her bandage. "Alice shot me."

"Fortunately, the bullet only creased your scalp, but it did give you a concussion and bled a lot. The doctors had to stitch you back up, but you're going to be fine." He squeezed her hand. "You scared the hell out of me, Lori. I thought for sure…" She saw him swallow. "I wish you would have told me you were going to see Alice."

"You were busy packing."

It was true. He'd planned to leave. He'd put the case behind him even though something had been nagging at him. "You hadn't been gone long when I got a call from one of the auto body shops that had fixed her damaged car after the hit-and-run. When I saw the photo of the car…"

"The senator didn't kill Billy," she said.

"No, he did apparently run over part of his body though and he didn't stop. Not to mention what he did to your mother. So he's still toast."

She nodded and felt her eyelids grow heavy. "I thought you might have already left."

He shook his head. "I'm not going anywhere. You rest. I'll be here."

Lorelei closed her eyes, hoping the next time she woke he wouldn't be gone and that this would have been nothing more than a sweet dream.

WILLIE COLT STOOD in the small second-floor office about to propose a toast. James had dug out a new bottle of blackberry brandy and paper cups.

"To my brother James," Willie said. "The first of the brothers to take his last ride."

There was laughter followed by rude remarks, but as James looked around the room at his brothers he'd never been happier. It had been so long since they'd all gotten together. "I've missed you guys." He still couldn't believe that they'd dropped everything and come running when he'd needed them.

The four of them had always been close, but definitely lived their own lives. They'd see each other at a rodeo here and there, but often went months without talking to each other. But when the chips were down, they always came through. They would squabble among themselves as boys, but if anyone else got involved, they stood together.

"You're really doing this?" Davey said, throwing an arm around his brother. "You're going to marry this woman?"

James nodded, grinning. "I really am. Well, I'm going to ask her to marry me. She hasn't said yes yet.

I thought I should wait until she's not doped up on the drugs they're giving her for the pain."

He'd been to the hospital every day. Lori was getting better. She was strong, just as he knew. She had bounced back fast and would be released from the hospital today.

"When are you going to ask her?" Davey wanted to know.

"I'm not sure. Soon, but I want to do it right, you know." He looked over at Tommy who'd wandered behind their father's desk and was now inspecting both James's and their father's private investigator licenses.

"You'll miss the rodeo," Davey predicted.

He couldn't deny it. "Not as much as I would miss Lori. I don't expect you to understand. I wouldn't have understood myself—until I fell in love."

Davey laughed. "I've been in love. It comes and goes. Mostly goes."

"I'm talking about a different kind of love other than buckle bunnies on the circuit," he said. "I can't even explain it. But you'll know it when it happens to you."

"So you're sticking with this PI gig?" Willie asked. "It sounds even more dangerous than bronc riding."

James chuckled. "Sometimes it definitely is. But I like it. I see why Dad liked it. Lori has her sandwich shop. Not sure what we'll do when we have kids."

"Wait a minute. *Kids?*" Davey said before the others could speak.

"She's not pregnant."

Willie chuckled. "You haven't even…"

"Nope. We literally haven't gotten that far." He

grinned. "But I know she'll want kids. I'm just hoping she'll want to start trying right after the wedding."

Willie was shaking his head. "Boy, when you fall, you fall hard. You sure about this?"

"I've never been more sure of anything," he said. He couldn't describe what it had felt like when he'd leaped out of his pickup and run toward Alice Sherman's car. The driver's side window had been blown out. There was blood everywhere. His knees had threatened to buckle under him when he'd realized that Lori had been shot.

"I'm thinking about building out on the ranch," he said. "There's plenty of room for all of us. As long as there are no objections." There were none. He knew that right now his brothers couldn't see themselves settling down. Eventually they would and the land would be there for them all.

"You going to keep the name, Colt Investigations?" Tommy asked. It was the first time he'd spoken since they'd come back from the hospital.

James studied him. "I guess, why?"

"Any chance you might want a partner?" his brother asked. Everyone turned to look at Tommy.

"Are you serious?" Davey sounded the most surprised. "You just turned thirty. You have a lot of rodeo ahead of you."

Tommy shook his head. "I've been thinking about quitting for some time now. I guess I was waiting for someone to go first." He smiled at James.

"You have even less experience at being a private

investigator than James," Willie pointed out. "No offense."

"It can't be that hard," Davey joked. "If James can do it."

"Right, nothing to it. James and Lorelei both almost got killed," Willie said, sounding genuinely worried.

But Tommy didn't seem to be listening. "Look at this office. I could start by getting it up to speed technologically." He continued, clearly warming to the subject. "We could invest in computers, an office landline, equipment and even filing cabinets."

James realized that his brother was serious. "You've given this some thought."

Tommy nodded. "I didn't work with Dad as much as you did, but I could learn on the job while I helped do whatever you needed done. Didn't you say a lot of the jobs you've been offered were small things like Dad used to do, finding lost pets, tracking cheating husbands and wives, filming people with work comp injuries Jet Skiing, that sort of thing. What do you say?"

"I actually think he's serious," Davey said with a shake of his head.

Willie had been watching them. "It sounds like a pretty good deal. We all know we can't rodeo forever."

"I say great," James said, surprised and yet delighted. He stepped to his brother and started to shake his hand, but instead pulled him into a bear hug. "Let's do this."

Willie was smiling broadly. "You could change the name to Colt Brothers Investigations."

"I like that," James said and looked to his brother. Tommy smiled and nodded. He looked at Willie and

Davey. "That way if the two of you ever—" Before he could get the words out, Davey stopped him.

"Not happening," Davey said. "I have big plans. None of them include getting myself shot at unless it's by an irate boyfriend as I'm going out a bedroom window."

They all laughed. Willie had been quiet. As James looked at him, his older brother winked at him. "Let's just see how it goes, but I know one thing. Dad would have loved this," he said, his voice breaking. He lifted his paper cup. "To Dad." They all drank and James refilled their cups.

"There is one more thing," James said. "One of the investigations I'll be working on involves Dad. I don't think his death was an accident." As he looked around the room at each of his brothers he saw that they'd all had their suspicions. "Maybe we can find out the truth."

"I'll drink to that," Davey said, and the rest raised their paper cups.

Chapter Twenty-Six

Lori looked forward to James's visits each day at the hospital. And each day she'd waited for him to tell her he was leaving. She knew she was keeping him in town and hated that he felt he had to stay because of her.

I'm fine, she'd told him yesterday when he'd come by. *I know you're anxious to get back on the rodeo circuit. Please don't stay on my account.*

I'm not going anywhere, he'd said. *I just spoke to the doctor. Told me that you're going to be released tomorrow. Which is good because I have a surprise for you.*

A surprise?

Yes, a surprise and no I'm not giving you any clues.

She'd been allowed to dress but had to wait for a wheelchair to take her down. She'd begun to worry that James wouldn't show up. Maybe that was the surprise, she'd been thinking when he walked in. She felt a wave of relief wash over her and felt herself smiling at just the sight of him.

He grinned. "Ready to blow this place?"

She nodded, a lump in her throat. He'd stayed for her. He had a surprise for her. She tried not to, but her heart filled like a helium balloon even as she warned herself 'that this was temporary. James never stayed anywhere long, and he'd been here way past time. Those boots of his would be itching to make tracks.

He wheeled her down to his pickup and helped her into the passenger seat. "I want to show you something," he said as he started the engine. "You feel okay, comfortable, need anything?"

She laughed. "I'm fine," she said as she buckled up her seat belt and settled in, wondering where he was taking her. "Still no clue as to this surprise of yours?"

James shook his head, still grinning. The radio was on to a Western station. Lorelei felt herself relax. She breathed in the warm summer air coming in through the open window. She was alive. Suddenly the world seemed bigger and brighter, more beautiful than she remembered—even the small town of Lonesome.

When she voiced her euphoric feeling out loud, James laughed and reached over to take her hand.

He gave it a squeeze, his gaze softening. "It sure seems brighter to me too, being here with you."

Lorelei felt her heart fill even more and float up. She felt giddy and as hard as she tried to contain her excitement, she couldn't as he headed out of town. She glanced over at him, again wondering where he was taking her.

He turned off onto a dirt road back into the pines and kept driving until the road ended on the side of a mountain overlooking the river. He stopped, cut the engine and turned toward her.

She wasn't sure what surprised her more, that he'd brought her here or that he seemed nervous.

"Do you like it?" he asked, his voice tight with emotion. She must have looked perplexed because he quickly added, "The view. I'm thinking about building a house on this spot. What do you think?"

She looked out at the amazing view. "It's beautiful." He was thinking about building a house here? This was the surprise? "How long have you been thinking about building here?"

"For a while now," he said. "Do you feel up to getting out? There is a spot close by I wanted to show you."

JAMES HAD NEVER been so nervous in his entire life. He'd climbed on the back of rank horses without breaking a sweat. He'd even ridden a few bulls he shouldn't have in his younger days. He'd been stomped and almost gored and still, he'd never hesitated to get back on.

But right now, as they walked through the wildflowers and tall summer grass toward his favorite spot, he felt as if he couldn't breathe.

He couldn't help being nervous. He'd planned out his life and Lori's and he wasn't even sure she wanted to marry him. They'd been through a lot in a short time. They'd gotten close. But they'd had only one date. One kiss.

It had been one humdinger of a kiss though, he thought with a grin.

As he walked, he reached into his pocket and felt the small velvet box. The engagement ring was an emerald, Lori's birthstone. The moment he'd seen it, he'd known it was perfect for her. He just hoped she liked it.

He took his hand out of his pocket, leaving the ring

in its box. He had to do this right, he thought as he glanced over at her. Her bandages had been removed all except for one. The headaches were only occasional and minor. The doctor had said that she was good to go.

"This isn't too much for you, is it?" James asked, his voice sounding tight.

Lori laughed. "I'm fine, James. Are you sure you're all right though?"

His laugh sounded even more nervous than he felt. He was glad when they reached the outcropping of rock. "This is my favorite spot."

"I can see why," she said, smiling up at him. "It's beautiful."

He reached down and picked a couple of wildflowers, held them in his fingers for a moment before he offered them to her. As she took them, he watched her expression soften. Her brown eyes seemed to turn golden in the summer sun. She was so beautiful that she took his breath away.

"Lori." He swallowed.

"James?" she asked, suspicion and concern in her voice.

"I'm in love with you." He spit out the words so quickly that he had to repeat them. "I'm madly in love with you." He waited for her reaction.

LORELEI COULDN'T HELP being shocked. He was looking at her as if he couldn't believe she really hadn't seen this coming.

"I brought you here because this is where I want to build our house. I know this is fast," he added quickly.

"And maybe out of the blue," she said, unable not to smile. "We've never even been on a real date."

"You didn't think dinner at the steak house was a real date? How about when we danced?"

She nodded and felt her cheeks warm. "That did feel like a date."

He grinned as if not as nervous as he'd been before. "How about when we kissed?"

She nodded as she felt color rising to her cheeks.

He cocked his head as he looked at her. "We packed a lot into a few weeks time, you and me. We solved a mystery together and almost got killed."

Chuckling, she said, "I suppose you could say we got to know each other."

His grin broadened. "I remember being in the closet with you."

She flushed and had to look away. "If that's your idea of courtship—"

"My idea of courtship is to spend every day loving you for the rest of my life."

"James, I know you feel responsible for what happened to the two of us and that's why you're saying this. But what about the rodeo?" she asked.

"I'm not asking you out of guilt, although I do feel responsible. I jumped into my father's case not realizing how many lives I was risking—especially yours. But over this time, you've changed me."

She couldn't help her skeptical look.

He laughed. "Changed me for the better. You've made me see what it is I want out of life. I want to be with you. When I almost lost you—"

"You didn't lose me. Once you realize that I'm fine, you can go back to the rodeo—"

"I'm not leaving. I figured I had maybe another year or two max. It was time, Lori. I love rodeoing, but I love you more."

Lorelei watched him drop to one knee. Reaching into his pocket, he came out with a small velvet box. "James?" She felt goose bumps ripple across her skin.

"Lorelei Wilkins? Will you marry me and make me the proudest man in the county?" he asked, his voice breaking.

"James."

"I want to go on dates with you, dance, kiss and make love. But I want to do it right. I want to do all of it with my wife. Say yes. You know you love me."

She laughed. "I do love you, Jimmy D."

He opened the small velvet box. "I saw this ring and it reminded me of you. One of a kind."

"My birthstone," she said. "Oh, James, it's beautiful." She met his gaze as tears filled her eyes. "Yes. Yes, I want to do all those things with you. As your wife."

He slipped the ring on her finger and rose to take her in his arms. The kiss held the promise of many days living on this mountainside overlooking the river. She could hear the laughter of their children, smell the sweet scents of more summers to come and feel James's arms around her always, sheltering her, loving her.

Chapter Twenty-Seven

Lorelei wanted to pinch herself as she stared into the full-length mirror at the woman standing there.

"You look beautiful," her stepmother said as she came up beside her. They smiled at each other in the mirror. "Such a beautiful bride."

"I'm doing the right thing," she said. "Aren't I? I know it's sudden. James and I hardly know each other."

"Hush," Karen said as she turned to her. "I've never seen anyone more in love than the two of you. You know James. And he knows you. I could see this coming for years. He was always trying to get your attention back in high school. You used to blush at just the sight of him."

"I still do," Lorelei confessed with a laugh. "It's the way he looks at me."

Her stepmother laughed. "I've seen it. It's the way every woman wants to be looked at. The way every woman wants to feel. You're very lucky."

"He makes me happy."

"I can see that." Karen looked at the time. "Ready?"

Lorelei took one last look at the woman in the mirror.

She was glowing, radiating happiness and excitement. Life with James would never be dull. Anita had offered to buy the sandwich shop. At first Lorelei had been surprised that her friend would think she wanted to sell it.

I just assumed you'd be working with James in the PI business until the babies start coming, Anita had said with a wink.

She'd laughed at the thought, but only for a moment. *James mentioned the same thing. He says he can't do it without me.*

When she'd mentioned selling the sandwich shop to James, he'd been excited to hear that she was going to do it. *We'll change the name of the business to Colt Investigations.*

No, Lorelei had said. *I think it should be Colt Brothers Investigations. I won't be working there. I'll be too busy. We have a wedding to plan, a house to build and decorate to get ready for the babies we're going to make.*

I do like the sound of that last part, he'd said with a laugh. *Let's get on that right after the wedding.* And he'd kissed her.

"Shall we do this?" her stepmother asked, bringing Lorelei out of her reverie.

Lorelei nodded. She couldn't wait.

The church was full to overflowing. Her three bridesmaids were ready. So were the three Colt brothers, but all she saw was James standing at the end of the aisle, waiting for her. The look in his eyes sent heat rocketing through her. Last night he'd told her about this vision he'd had of a little girl of about two on a horse.